SHOWKEN

THE DRAGLEN BROTHERS SERIES

By Solease M Barner

Publishing
Covers & Formatting
http://paradoxbooktrailerproductions.blogspot.com.au

Copyright © 2013 by Solease M Barner

ISBN-13: 978-1493759217

ISBN-10: 1493759213

Editing: Tabitha Ormiston-Smith

All rights reserved.

THANK YOU

I have to thank all my readers, who support me in my writing. I appreciate all the love for this new series. I feel very blessed when I encounter many of you on my website, Facebook, emails, and even in public. I hope to encounter more of you in the future.

I hope you enjoy the second book in the series, readers!

I must thank a few people individually:

Kera Montgomery, you are awesome. I'm so happy to have you as a supporter. I am honored to have your support. I truly appreciate all your work!

Denise Bush you are a rock star! I'm so glad to have you a part of my team. Thank you for supporting me. Thanks for the gifts you make for my books, they are special to me. I love the necklace, it's fabulous! I'm happy you enjoy my books, and hope you enjoy SHOWKEN!

Karen Henderson you are like a machine, you just keep promoting my books, and for that I say thank you. I appreciate all your hard work and hope you continue to support me.

I have to thank my wonderful group, my Beautiful Divas, I love each and every one of you! I hope Showken is what you all expect.

There are so many of you who go out of your way for me, I can't name you all, but know I love you all! I look forward to getting feedback on this series from you all!

The Special People working on the book to make it perfect:

Tabitha Ormiston-Smith, you know how to make a girl work. We've done it again, another book completed!! Whooohoo!! You are the best editor I've encountered. You were less evil during the editing this time, which means I'm learning! I know I can say that to you. I always say to myself, Tabitha and I are in a love/hate relationship. I know when you are angry when I see caps in comments on edits. I also know when something made you giggle as well. I appreciate you teaching me to be better at writing, and keeping my feet to the fire. I love working with you and look forward to more books together!

Patti Roberts, you are full of talent! I look forward to doing covers with you. The way you bring life to my vision on a cover is amazing. SHOWKEN's cover is HOT!!! I'm like a kid in a candy store when I know we are working on covers. You're always so patient with me, very accommodating, and kind. ☺ I always say you're heaven sent, and I mean that. I can't wait to work with you, it's such a joy to spend time working on covers with you, even when I ask for changes after I've said 'I love it', you change it without complaint, and for that I thank you deep down.

Beta Readers

I LOVE YOU ALL!! I truly enjoy how you are all so truthful with me about my books. I won't give names, because I like to keep my beta readers to myself! You all know who you are, my first readers. I always look forward to your feedback. You are all awesome!

SPECIAL THANKS

I'm not ashamed and will always thank my heavenly father Jesus Christ. I would not even be here without Him. I have to thank my wonderful husband. I'm so blessed to share my life with you. I love that you are so accepting of my madness, when writing, editing, promoting, and the crazy schedule I have, still you never complain. To my precious daughter, Mommy loves our time together. I love that smile and how we can talk about anything. You will always be my baby. Thank you Mom and Dad, for supporting me with all the wisdom you give me. I love you both, and consider it a blessing to have you as parents. I love all my sisters and love each one of you for being there for me no matter what. Shatina, my manager, I love you so much; you always make sure I stay focused, reminding me of all the important things, and pushing out the negative. Thank you. To my nephew/son, I love talking with you. You are so wise at such a young age, your advice is appreciated. To Nikki, you are the best P.A. and I'm not ever letting you go. To my friend who is awesome, I love reading books with you and discussing our fictional boyfriends, you know who you are, SWH!!! LOL. To the best book club ever, I love all of you and enjoy our meetings, with such great food and wine! If I have missed anyone please don't charge it to my heart. I love all my family and friends!

Solease M Barner.

GLOSSARY

Aumdo (*n*) - The Laws, written in book form for dragons.

Cortamagen (*n*) - The land where the Draglen brothers live.

Cati (*adj*) - Foolish, silly.

Dorli (*ejac*) - I apologize.

Giver (*n*) - A man or woman chosen by one of the Draglen Descendants to fulfil his or her sexual needs; the position approximates to that of a kept mistress.

Hulin (*n*) - A cliff that belongs to Draglen Dragons.

Kalin (*n*) - The planet on which Cortamagen is located.

Key (*n*) -A human who keeps a portal open for dragons to travel from their land to Earth. Not all humans have this ability.

Leka (*n*) - A loyal friend.

Magen (*n*) - The language of Cortamagen.

Molla (*n*) - The male mate in Kalin.

Taker (*n*) - A dragon who has taken a Giver.

Wella (*n*) -The female mate in Kalin.

Youngs (*n*) -Children.

Zell (*n*) - Beloved.

ALWAYS MINE!

I thought I had more time,

But then, I laid eyes on you,

And thought, she sure is fine

Even made up in my mind how to make you mine!

Yet, you wouldn't even let me take you out to dine.

I was persistent though, I knew you just needed time.

I even crossed the line and almost lost you,

For not using my mind,

Yet, here we are together

Standing,

Shining forever!

Always Mine!

SHOWKEN

Why the hell did Draken choose me to run the business? Damn. If I'm running it, then human women are allowed in the car, house, and definitely the office. I'm happy Layern and Hawken are coming along. Gemi decides to stay, but Domlen decided he would come, also.

"Okay, I'm in charge now and I say there are no rules, except don't expose us or I will be fucking pissed," I say. Layern ignores me. Hawken and Domlen just look.

"You're not running shit," Hawken says.

"I run everything," I say, "and unlike Draken, I will burn your ass, and that will take months to heal. Now, who's up for a drink at a bar I've been dying to go to?"

"I'm up for it. What's the name of the bar?" Domlen says, not looking up from his laptop.

"Hot Chicks and Drinks," Layern says, looking serious. I have to make sure Layern gets laid. Domlen and Hawken and I have nothing to worry about.

"Well lets go see what's in the Hot Chicks and Drinks Bar. I think this might be my lucky day."

I go to my room to get ready. I love human women, and plan on bringing at least two home tonight. I just don't like when they get all "Showken, you going to call," or "Showken, I think I love you," to hell with that. I don't want that shit. I just want a good lay, and to keep it moving. I may settle down in about, oh, another hundred years, but right now I'm having fun. I walk back, Domlen and Layern are ready. Hawken hasn't bothered to change.

"Okay, no hurting the human women. If they say no, respect it and move on. Don't start any fights, as we have to go to work on Monday. Please, don't fall in love like Draken, he went crazy. Now he is hooked on Cess. I don't have time for a repeat." I grab the keys to the Hummer.

"Showken, stop giving out orders, you sound like Draken. He always wants to give out orders," Hawken says. We all laugh.

"Yeah, but now Cess is giving the orders," Domlen says. Layern shakes his head.

"Let's just go have some fun. Look, we're already here," Hawken says.

2

We all walk into the bar, and it's pretty packed, but it's Friday. I'm casing the place, and see her behind the bar placing drinks on a tray. She has dark brown hair, hanging straight. Her body has all the right curves. Yes, she is going to be one of them tonight. She looks mad, but I'll just smile. She will melt and the panties will be off.

"I'm going to get a waitress for us, go find a table," I say, heading straight for her.

"Stop giving out orders!" Hawken yells out. I ignore his jealous ass and keep moving until I'm right in front of her.

"Excuse me. My brothers and I need our order to be taken," I say, hoping she will look up. Instead, she keeps placing drinks on the tray to deliver.

"So fucking what. Wait your turn," she says, and moves around me, walking toward another table. Shit. This one has some issues. It doesn't matter. I still want to have her in my bed tonight. I walk to our table, and sit. She walks over with a small pad and pen.

"What can I get you boys?"

"Boys?" Domlen says, "You see any boys?"

"As a matter of fact, yes. Now what you want to drink?"

Oh, she is really angry. I like it.

"We would like some pitchers of beer, the best you have," Layern says.

"Is that all?" she asks, not looking at any of us. I wonder what that's all about. She can't be shy with a mouth like that. Hmmm…

3

"Yes, I would like to know what time you're off?" I ask, trying to get her to look at me. She finally does. There are those beautiful grey eyes. She is one angry lady, but I like her. She could be fun.

"Look, I'm not interested. I'll be back with the beer," she says, walking away. I watch her sexy walk, back to the bar counter to get our orders. She is a woman. Her ass, breasts, and hips are perfect.

"Showken, I think you should leave this one alone. She is very good at blocking emotion, but I was able to sense that she is very angry and damaged," Layern says.

"I think you guys can talk about this, I've spotted my fun for tonight," Hawken says, heading over to a table with a couple of ladies. They look fun, all smiles, but I want her. She basically said 'fuck off' to me, and that is not happening.

"She's an angry human female, but she is not allowed to call me boy again, or she'll-" Domlen says, just as our pitchers arrive. She sets them down with glasses, and I slide a hundred towards her.

"Here's your beer, and is this to start a tab?" she snaps.

"Nope, it's your tip for being so nice," I say, giving her a wicked smile. She is angry, huh? Well, I will see if she is really not into me, or just too scared to admit it. I notice she just stares at me, and we do this staring thing for a good ten seconds before she blinks.

"I'll start your tab," she says, snatching the money and

4

walking away.

"I see that Hawken is having a good time, I'm going to claim myself some fun, too." Domlen says, pouring himself a glass and taking a pitcher with him, heading towards Hawken and the women.

"Layern, what is it about her?" I ask, not taking my eyes off her as she takes orders and delivers them.

"You shouldn't, but since she gave you a challenge, I see you will stop at nothing to have her, just be careful." Layern takes a long gulp. "I'm going to dance and have some fun, too. I think you should come too. I see those women on the floor dancing our way, they are waiting for us," he says, rising, and moving closer to the dancing floor, which is not very big, but big enough.

"I'll join you in a second, get them warm and I'll be over to relieve you of one," I say, smiling, knowing Layern is good at dancing. He can handle two or three human women at once. Layern walks away shaking his head. I continue staring at her. I need her name. I walk to the bar, blocking her from going behind it.

"What the hell you doing?" she yells at me, trying to go around. I just smile, and wait for her to look at me. Finally her head rises to meet mine. She is beautiful, even angry.

"What's your name?"

"I'm not telling you my name. You're more than likely a stalker as you can't take a hint already," she snaps, placing her hands on those lovely hips. "Now move!" She looks me dead in the eyes, but I see a guard up, not anger. Huh, I need to know more.

"I'm Showken. You are . . ." I say, raising a brow. She is not getting past without a name.

"Marilyn, now can you move?" she says through her teeth.

"That wasn't hard, Marilyn, and yes, I will move, for now," I say, stepping aside and making sure to feel her heat as she slides past me, trying not to touch. I stand and listen as she gives the bartender her order for another table. She looks pissed, but I still want her. She just has to be difficult, and I love a challenge. She turns and looks at me, rolling her beautiful eyes. Oh, yes, this one I will have. I return a wide smile, and head for the dance floor. I pull the first girl I see out of her seat, and dance with her seductively. The lady is very willing and aroused, but my eye is on Marilyn as she watches the show. I sniff the air, and there it is; she is hot. She likes my dancing. I make eye contact with her, then we just stare at each other, and I mouth "I want you," licking my lips for her pleasure. I really need this woman. I see Domlen and Hawken walk out with their fun for tonight. Smiling, I nod to them. The song ends, and Layern meets me at the table.

"Showken, what is it about her? I'm picking up anger and arousal, but the anger is way more intense. The human you were just dancing with is willing to do whatever with you," Layern says, drinking straight from the only pitcher left. I smile, knowing she has to come back.

"Marilyn!" I yell, forcing her to look again. She looks sexy as hell walking this way. I may just want her because she said no. Whatever the reason, I can't help but rise to the challenge. Finally getting to our table, she places her hands on her hips, narrowing beautiful grey eyes at me.

"We need more pitchers," I say, raising my brow and sliding another hundred dollar bill her way. She snatches again, and storms off without a word. She says nothing, heading for the bar.

"You are really pissing her off," Layern says, finishing the pitcher.

"I know, that's the point. She's very angry, very hot, too. I think a little fun will help her out," I say, not taking my eyes off her as she brings four pitchers back to the table. I wonder does she think she can get me drunk? She bangs them down, spilling some, and storms off angrily. I tilt my head, watching her walk away is amazing.

"Layern, I'm not giving up on this one. After I have my fun I'll leave her alone," I say, grabbing a pitcher, and taking a huge gulp.

"Ok, but I'm telling you, this one is not for fun. She has secrets that I can't get to. I'd stay clear if I were you, but seeing the sparkle in your eye, brother, I know you will stop at nothing. So good luck."

"Luck? Shit, I plan on having a good time with Ms Marilyn," I say. "Her anger only excites me. Besides, I don't think she knows how angry I can get." I watch her maneuver through the crowd delivering beers.

She ignores me for the rest of the night. Layern invites some ladies to the table, and they are very willing, but I can't keep my eyes off her. I give attention to the redhead purring next to me, but I don't want an easy lay tonight. I want a challenge, and I see I have one. Studying her walk, how she stands, her eyes, I smile, thinking it will be fun getting to know her. She shakes her head every time she looks my way, sighing in frustration. Yes, I'm in her mind, now I want in that body of hers.

"I'm going home, brother. You coming?" Layern says, standing with a lady on his arm. I stare at him in confusion, I know who already holds my brother's heart. Maybe he's over her.

"I think I'll make sure Marilyn gets home safe, but you have some fun with both," I say, leaning over and giving the redhead next to me a kiss. "Sweetheart, you and your friend will take care of my brother, right?" I smile, and she melts.

"Yes, of course," she says, rising. Layern takes her arm, and they all go for the door. It's getting late. I will stay until she leaves. I need to see what I'm up against.

MARILYN

I wish this guy would just leave. Shit, I don't have time for this crap. If he thinks throwing his money around is going to get him laid, then he is out of his mind. I hate when these rich asses come in the bar, and assume, because I work at a bar, that I'm desperate. Please.

I can't wait to get home and soak my feet. I've been working all day; leaving my first job at the gas station, and coming to the bar with only an hour break, my jobs can really wear me out. Glancing at his table, I see his friend is leaving, and he is staring at me, again, with those fucking amazing eyes. I don't care if he waits. If he harasses me when I get off work, which is in about twenty minutes, I'm going to kick him right in the balls.

"Marilyn!" I hear Jasmine call my name. I turn, and she is looking at him.

"Yes, Jasmine?" I ask, watching her stare at him.

"Who is that hot, sexy man staring at you?" Jasmine asks, licking her lips and rubbing her hand up her neck. Is this loser turning her on, really?

"Some guy who can't take 'no' for an answer. If you want him, go at it, I'm not giving him the time of day or night," I say, watching her mouth move. No words are coming out. "Jasmine, snap out of it! Geez, he's just a guy, a very hot guy, but still a guy who probably just wants a roll in the hay, or maybe even in the car. Jasmine? Jasmine, are you listening to me?" I ask, shaking her arm.

"Yes, I'm listening to you. I would have him if I could. Shit, I would even share him with you, but looks like he only has eyes for you," she says, smiling. Jasmine is my only friend. I don't have any brothers or sisters. My father is in prison, and my mother should be in prison. I'm not easy to get along with, yet Jasmine can always make me smile.

"Well, Jazz, you don't have to share, he's all yours. Maybe he'll leave me alone, and stop staring at me. It's uncomfortable having his eyes roam my body," I say, shivering.

"Marilyn, listen, when was the last time you had sex? Before you answer, remember I've been your friend for at least two years, and you never come into work talking about a steamy night. So, look at the hot guy again, and ask yourself: do you really want to pass up a very handsome, sexy man who is staring at you like you are freaking awesome?" Jasmine asks excitedly. I roll my eyes at her, and she shakes her head, walking behind the bar.

"I'm going home now, my shift is over. I don't want to talk to him. Besides, you know he would not want me, anyway," I say, going over to the bar to count my tips.

"Who says it's a relationship? It's just sex, you can have that. Don't tell him anything, just have sex."

"Nope, have a good night, Jazz," I say, waving to Jimmy, the bartender and owner. I walk out of the back of the bar, hoping he thinks I'm in the bathroom and doesn't follow me. I push open the door, and the night air is awesome, it has cooled down some. I get to go home, soak my feet and sleep in tomorrow. It's my day off from both jobs. I begin the walk to my Ford Taurus, and I see him next to my car. Stopping to make sure my gun is tucked behind me, I see him leaning on my car, looking very sexy, but he could be a stalker.

"Get away from my car, you creep," I yell, hoping he goes about his business.

"I'm not going to hurt you, I just want to get to know you," he yells back. I take in a slow deep breath, and start walking to my car. It's the weekend, and the parking lot is packed. I arrived late, so I parked pretty far away. If he tries anything I'm going to give him one in the knee.

"I don't have time to talk," I whisper to myself. Finally

reaching my car, I get a good look at his body, he is built freaking awesome. He is towering over me with his frame; his hair is blond, long and gorgeous. His eyes are deep green and his smile is to die for. Shit, I've not described a guy like that to myself in a long time.

"I don't want to hurt you, Marilyn, I don't want anything from you at all," he smiles, and his eyes are moving very slowly down my body, coming back up to meet my eyes. My mouth is dry, and out of nowhere, I feel arousal. "I would like to give you pleasure, as I see you are full of anger and if I can help just a little . . ." he trails off. I'm pretty sure my face is red. He just fucked me with his damn sexy eyes.

"I'm going home, alone," I say, waiting for him to step aside. He does. I feel his hand on the lower part of my back when I open the door to get in the car.

"Mmmm, you smell good, I bet you taste better. Will you let me have a taste?" he asks, right in my ear with a very seductive voice. I'm not giving in to a stranger.

"I'm going home now," I say, climbing in, and he shuts my door. I start the car, snatching my seat belt, and I see him watching me very closely. I should be scared, but I'm not. I can handle myself, and if not, George, my .45 caliber, is more than happy to help me any time. I pull away, looking in my mirror, and he is still watching. I'm not sure, but I think he mouths, 'I want you,' again to me. I shake it off, and get on the freeway heading to West Phoenix where I live. I live in a one-bedroom apartment with my best friend, Bruiser. Bruiser is my Rottweiler, and I love him to death. He never asks anything of me, and he is the only one I feel comfortable around, no matter what. I get excited to get home to him, and drive a little faster.

***

That was such a great bath. I walk slowly toward the kitchen for a snack before I turn in for the night. As I'm looking in the fridge, I see nothing I truly want, so I settle for some left-over tuna fish. Bruiser and I head to my room, where he lies at my feet while I get comfy for some late night T.V. As I'm flipping through the channels, I hear my neighbors having sex. The wall behind my bed is shaking. I hate these thin walls. I turn up the movie, and continue to watch. My mind goes back to that guy at the bar. What did he say his name is? Showlem? Showhen? No Showken. Yes, that's his name, Showken. He sure is a good-looking man. If I wasn't such a mess, I might have taken him up on his offer, but I'm no good for him or anyone. I'm eating my tuna and crackers, and Showken is still popping into my head with his intense green eyes. I mean, who has eyes like that? I'm trying my hardest to go to sleep, but it doesn't arrive, so I decide to get out my B.O.B., and release some stress. I got Mr. Longfellow from a Pure Romance party Jasmine had a few months ago. Closing my eyes I see Showken and his smile, that instantly has me horny. Bruiser is asleep, so I spread my legs, sliding in Mr. Longfellow as I visualize Showken. Ahhh, that feels so good. I adjust the speed and go to the highest level. My hips are moving, and boy does this feel amazing. Ohhhh . . . mmm, I see his green eyes, hear his voice, smell his cologne and I'm over the cliff. "Yes, yessssss. Ohhhh, yes!" I find myself panting afterwards, needing more, wishing it really were Showken. What has this man done to me? I close my eyes, and soon sleep finds me.

***

Thank heavens I have today off. It's been forever since I had a day off from both jobs. I'm not going anywhere. I'm staying in my pajamas and relaxing today. I decide to cook myself a real breakfast instead of the on-the-go bars I usually eat. Today, I'm cooking blueberry pancakes, eggs with cheese and some crispy bacon. I'm not worried about calories today; it's all about me. I drift back to my night, seeing his eyes staring at me, and a slight moan escapes, "Mmmm." Shit, Marilyn, get yourself together. He doesn't really want you; he was probably so drunk he didn't realize what he was saying. After I fix Bruiser some breakfast, I finish cooking and sit at my tiny table. I eat in silence, and a feeling of disappointment comes over me. 'It was nice to have Showken pursuing you', my subconscious says. I'm drawn from my thoughts of last night when my cell rings.

"Hello, Jasmine," I say, stuffing my mouth.

"Marilyn, guess who came in last night after you left, and wanted to know when you are working?"

"Tell me you didn't."

"I so fucking did, and I even gave him your address," Jasmine says. Why the hell would she do that, he could be a stalker or worse.

"Jasmine, why did you think it was okay to do that? I mean he-" before I can finish, she cuts me off, talking again.

"Listen, I did some digging, and that is not just some regular guy, that's Showken Draglen from Out of World Enterprises. Sweetie, that, my dear, is better than awesome," Jasmine is very excited, and one horny lady. She is 25 years old with a 3 year-old daughter. She was drunk when she got pregnant and can't remember who the father is, which makes her a single parent. Rachel is my god-daughter and I love her, so it's like Jasmine and I share her.

"Jasmine! Oh Jasmine, I don't care who he is. I'm not seeing him, and you shouldn't have given him my address. As much as I'd like to be pissed, I can't stay mad at you for long. I hope he doesn't come to my place, for your sake," I say, stuffing my mouth with more food.

"I hope he does. I mean you and your B.O.B. are too well acquainted, it's time for the real thing, and I think Showken Draglen wants to rock your world. I mean, I did throw myself at him, and he turned me down like a perfect gentleman, meaning he wants you," she says, enthusiastically. I hear Rachel playing in the background, and it makes me smile. I used to wish for children when I was a little girl; now, I pray I never have one.

"Jasmine, he better not show up at my door. I'm not kidding; you know how I feel about strangers coming to my house. If he gets shot I'm blaming you," I say, walking my empty plate over to the sink.

"If that sexy man shows up at your door with the body and smile he has, you need to invite him in and show him to the bedroom," she says. I can picture her silly grin right now.

"I won't do that, thanks for giving a stranger my address! I'm going to sit and relax, give Rachel a kiss for me," I say.

"Anytime, and I will give her a kiss for you, bye, Marilyn."

"Bye, Jazz," I say, ending the call. I plop down on my sofa, and turn on the television. I begin watching, and the next thing I know I fall asleep. A knock at the door wakes me up. I get up, and see it's just after noon. Wow, I was really tired. I walk slowly to the door and open it without thinking. His fragrance hits me like a ton of bricks. I raise my head slowly, meeting his gaze, and instantly my body reacts to his intense stare and green eyes.

"Hello, Marilyn," he says. His smile is captivating. I'm lost for words, and struggle to gain composure.

"Umm, umm, why are you here?" I ask, admiring him in his sexy slacks and casual shirt. He looks amazing, but I still don't want him.

"I got your address from your friend Jasmine, and was wondering if you would be more likely to see me outside the bar. I would like to take you to lunch," he says, turning his smile into a very seductive look.

"I don't think that's a good idea, Showken," I say, fixing my t-shirt over my pajama pants.

"Oh, Marilyn, I think it's a great idea, and I love that you remember my name," he says, looking over my shoulder. "What is the name of your dog?" he asks. I see Bruiser in the corner watching us. Shit, he doesn't know Showken, Bruiser should be barking his ass off right now. He and I will have a talk later about my protection.

"That's Bruiser, and I'm still not going to lunch with you. Besides, I hear you're some hot-shot businessman; why do you want me, anyway?" I ask, giving him a serious look. I don't understand why he is pursuing me so hard, and I don't want to find out.

"Marilyn, I'll wait for you to get dressed, besides it's just lunch, and I'm not a hot-shot businessman; I'm more of a hot-flaming beast," he says, putting emphasis on beast. He pushes past me, despite my protest, and sits on my sofa. He is so huge my sofa looks like a mini sofa with him on it. "Bruiser, come sit with me," he says, and Bruiser, my best friend and guard dog, betrays me and sits at his feet. What the hell?

"Look," I say, placing my hands on my hips, while trying to control my attraction to this guy. "If the only way to get you out of my house is to go to lunch, then I'll go, but you have to promise to leave me alone afterward." The last man I was with sexually was a year ago and it lasted maybe ten minutes.

"Marilyn, lunch is just the beginning."

17

We stare at each other, and I get lost in those eyes. I turn and storm into my room. My first thought is to snatch my gun, but I walk past my nightstand, and jump in the shower for my unwanted lunch date.

SHOWKEN

"Bruiser, you are such a good boy," I say to her dog. He responds by rubbing his head against my leg for a pat. This Marilyn is such a challenge, but I smelled her sex as soon as I came to her door. Layern wants me to leave her alone, but I can't. I need this woman under me, begging me for more. She is so stubborn and I want her badly; I will have her.

She walks out of the bathroom after forty-five minutes, looking amazing. She has on a white tank with a pair of jeans. She has her hair down, and my mouth opens as she enters. I smell coconut oozing from her. I smile and she rolls her eyes, but I caught her slight smile. She likes the attention.

"Marilyn, you look - and smell - amazing, let's get something to eat," I say, standing.

"Showken, remember what I said after we eat lunch," she says. I shake my head, arching a brow at her.

"You know I'm not listening to you, right," I say, laughing. We go to the door, and I let her lead, so I can look at that ass walking in front of me. Yes, she will be in my bed.

"You remember, or else," she says. I stop her by pulling at her arm, and she tries to snatch away. "Keep your hands off me or lunch is off," she snarls at me. Shit, she can growl. I really like her now.

"There will never be an 'or else' with me, like I said, I just want to get to know you in every way. Oh, I love the almost growl you did, also. I hope to hear that again, under different circumstances," I say, waving my hand towards the car.

"You, driving?" she asks, shocked.

"Oh, you thought I would have a driver, well I told you I'm a hot-flaming beast and I don't need a driver, bodyguard or anything else to survive in this country," I say, opening the door to my Hummer. She climbs in, looking at me strangely. and then her arousal hits me again.

I really didn't want to do lunch; I just want her in my bed. When I get her in my bed, I'm so going to taste her all night long. That body wash and her natural juice are driving me insane, my beast is going crazy. I would hate to use my powers on her, this woman I will have.

"I know a great Mexican restaurant nearby that we could go

to," she says. I feel her anxiety.

"Marilyn, calm down, I promise you that nothing will happen to you," I say, smelling the gun she's carrying. "I'm much better protection than the gun you carry, angel."

"I don't like to be called names that aren't mine."

"Okay, precious," I say, chuckling, oh I can't wait to get you naked, Marilyn. We drive off, and she gives me directions to this restaurant she's talking about. We get inside and order all sorts of food, well, I order all sorts of Mexican dishes, she settles for enchiladas. I watch her eat, and she watches me for a few minutes, should I see why she's so angry, before I have her?

"So, tell me, what is it that has you angry at the world?" I ask, putting down my fork and giving her my undivided attention. Her grey eyes narrow slightly.

"I'm not angry at the world, just at stalkers who don't know how to leave a girl alone," she says, taking a sip of her Coke. I nod, letting her believe that she will get away with that answer.

"I'm not a stalker, I just know that we can have some fun. I'm not asking for your hand in marriage, just one night of hot, sweaty sex," I say, staring her in the eyes, giving her no chance to look away. I see the blood rush straight to her cheeks. I continue to stare and she blinks a few times, caught off guard by my forwardness.

I really have stepped out of my comfort zone. Tracking a girl down just to sleep with her is not my style. I have never been rejected, and Marilyn is not getting off that easily. She has the body of a goddess, and sex appeal surrounding her. I lick my lips.

Just visualizing her rocking in my bed instantly gets me hard.

"Showken, it's not gonna happen, please stop. You're wasting your time with me; I'm not that girl. I think . . . I think I will be catching the bus home." She rises to leave, and I panic.

"Please, don't embarrass me. I drove you here and I will drive you home, if that is what you wish," I say, sighing as she sits back down. I entwine my fingers together in front of me. My anger with this woman is at another level right now. I'm not used to this, and she thought she was going to catch a bus home. What type of guy does she think I am? "I don't know what or who has hurt you, Marilyn, but I would like to get to know you better, even if only as friends. You intrigue me, and that has not happened in a very long time. I won't ask for sex, if you spend time with me, deal?" I ask. If she thinks I'm going to let her go, she doesn't know me, my beast hits me inside and I feel a need to release.

Maybe if I can find out the problem with her anger I can get what I want. This wouldn't be a problem if I took on a Giver, except I don't want one. I've always had many women, with a Giver, a bond can form, making you only react to her. I could never see myself with one woman like Draken. Cess has him wrapped around her finger. I'm never getting that involved, not for a long time. I hope she accepts my offer, for I really want to feel her body.

"Why would you want to spend time with me as a friend?" she asks, looking shocked.

"I told you. You intrigue me and I would like to know you

better. Besides, I don't have any friends, and you seem like you need a friend like I do," I say, giving her a look that I know she likes, as her arousal reaches my nose. I tense, knowing I could throw her on top of the table right now.

"I'm not in need of friends, Showken. I appreciate the lunch, but I would like to go home now," she says, looking me in the eyes. I see past all the anger and hurt, I know she needs me.

"Okay, I'll take you home," I say, leaving a fifty on the table and waiting for her to stand.

"You know, you are generous with tips," she says, eyeing the fifty on the table.

"In my land, giving is what we do. In your land, giving is done only for tax breaks," I say, giving her my full smile. I see her hesitation as I wave for her to walk in front, but I have to see that nice, firm ass.

"What country are you from?" she asks, glancing back. She catches me looking at her ass, fuck.

"A place you haven't heard of. Hey, how about we go for a walk in the park?" I ask, diverting her question. My land is not up for discussion.

"Umm, I want to go home, remember I said 'no' to the friend thing," she says. I hold open the restaurant door for her, walking her to my Hummer.

"Oh, yeah, you did say that. We're talking now, and I think I see a very small smile coming across your face. Yes, there it is," I say, watching as she can't help but smile. She is beautiful. She is not a piece of steel, just wounded. "What a beautiful smile you have, Marilyn, and I'm saying it as a friend," I say, opening the door and watching her perfect body climb into my vehicle.

"You are pushy, but I just want to go home and spend time with Bruiser," she says. "That's my friend, and sometimes Jasmine, whom I might take back my friendship since she gave you my address." I stand there holding her door open, but I really want to lean in and give her a long kiss. Instead, I use some of my heat and push it out of my body, sending it right to hers, giving her a really good, warm feeling everywhere. I finally close the door and drive her back to her tiny apartment. She jumps out fast, but not fast enough. I reach her just as she shuts her door.

"What, no hug?" I ask, watching her response and knowing she wants to. She is fighting this hard.

"Showken," she says, shaking a finger at me. "One hug, then you leave and never come to my place uninvited again." Shit, I'm not agreeing to any such thing. I make my way towards her until I am very close to her, without touching, I tilt my head, then very slowly place my hands on her hips and pull her to me fast. Slowly moving my hands up her back, leaning my head into her neck, I softly place a kiss, and I hear the moan leave her mouth. "Mmmm." She is not going to get rid of me. Besides, her body betrays her and I know she wants me, too.

"Have a good day, Marilyn," I say, walking away. I jump into my Hummer and drive away. I see she is running her hand through her hair. She wants me. I head home, trying to calm my beast, relaxing my body from wanting to pin her down and make her admit her attraction to me. I smile, thinking of all the ways I can do that. "I'll see you later, Marilyn."

***

I'm sitting in the study, having a drink, when Domlen and Hawken come in laughing. They stop when they see me, and smile.

"What?" I ask, knowing they know I went to find Marilyn.

"You're not smiling, so that means she still said no," Hawken says, pouring a drink for himself and sitting in front of me.

"Hawken, you know I'm not Draken, I'll fuck you up," I say, giving him a huge smile. My brothers know I have an ugly side that none of them ever wants out, but Hawken is the brother who always has to say something. I look over at Domlen, he's just sitting and watching us, saying nothing, but I see his smirk. I shake my head and take another drink.

Shit, Domlen can't say anything with the way he gets his women. Fuck him, too. All she had to do was say yes and I would not be justifying why I'm going to have to be her unwanted friend to have sex with her. Closing my eyes, I think of her naked. Yes, it will be worth it, I say to myself. Layern comes strolling in with a smile; looks like my brother had a good time. I'm glad, he needs to get over her. I smile.

"Layern, looks like you were treated right last night," I say, watching the joy come back into my brother.

"And this morning. I almost forgot how good a human woman could feel. Almost," Layern says, pouring a nice-sized drink and sitting in the chair next to me. Domlen's and Hawken's mouths are open. I just can't stop smiling. Layern is back. Yes, I miss having my brother who goes after what he wants. Every other one of my brothers has had a Giver, or they still do. Layern and I have always chosen to stay away from that.

"Layern, why didn't you show us?" Hawken asks. I frown, only now realizing he didn't show us.

"Yes, I would have loved to see my brother come back," I say.

"Well, I was nervous at first, not knowing if I could, as it's been a while, but once I got going I forgot to show anybody anything. Besides, if you had tapped into my mind, I would have let you all in. You would have had a chance to see those girls having a good time."

"You seeing them again?" Domlen asks.

"No, you know I never adapted to that twice thing, only once . . . anyway, enough about me. Showken," Layern says, turning to look me in the eye. "How is Marilyn coming along for you?"

"Damn, you know I've never had a woman tell me no. That shit is pissing me off. Then, she even had the nerve to say she doesn't want to be my friend. I mean, I'm a great friend to have, ask Cess," I say, drifting back into my desire for Marilyn.

"I say move on," Domlen says. "Besides, brother, if you need a woman I can make a call and you will get every need met, no strings attached. I promise," he says. I don't want any of his women. Doesn't he know I don't like anything my brothers have had?

"Domlen, I want her and I will have her. Now, has anyone gone over the files for next quarter?" I say, changing the subject. For the rest of the day we are all business. When night falls, I decide that maybe I'm being too soft. Should I forget about rejection, or should I take it as motivation? Well, since I am a predator and Marilyn is running, it just makes it more fun to catch her. I will continue to pursue her and win. When I catch her she's going to want more. After dinner I head to my room and lie on my bed, just as my phone starts ringing. Ahh, Draken, of course.

"Hello brother, you should not be calling, you should be trying to give us some Youngs."

"I'm working on it, Princess is asleep right now. I'm calling to see if you guys are doing alright with the company, without me there," Draken says, leaving no doubt about why he really called.

"Yes, the business is going to be fine. In fact, we had a great meeting. We discussed Layern's women he had over last night, and how he is back now!" I say, grinning. I know Draken does not like us playing around, but he's married to what he was supposed to play with. I feel him wanting to get pissed about it, and even hear his growl, now it's silence. I chuckle, knowing he won't risk waking up Cess.

"Showken, one of these days . . . fuck! Okay, I'm glad to hear you are at least taking care of business," Draken says.

"Why wouldn't I? It's the family business, and family means

27

everything to me," I say. I hate it when Draken checks up on me to see if I'm doing a good job on tasks, but I know he means well. I love my brother and would die for him; I want to make him proud, always.

"I trust you, Showken, now tell me about Layern," Draken says, enthusiastically. We have all hoped Layern would find his way back to sex, as he is totally addicted to it. But since his heart was shattered, he's been on this five-year strike, only seeking oral sex when the pressure is too much and he has to release.

"Well, we went to this bar last night, and I saw the girl I wanted, but she's playing hard to get. I had a very willing human female and so did Layern, but since I wanted Marilyn, I gave Layern an extra. He walked into the study today like a new man, and it felt good to see our brother smile. Draken, he's back," I say, smiling. All of us have been waiting for Layern to get his smile back. Now that he has it, look out everyone. He's more of a player than me.

"Whoa, who is Marilyn? You never remember a human name, and did you say she said no?" Draken asks. I knowingly smile. I said all of that and he only heard my comment about Marilyn.

"Draken, don't worry about me, I'm telling you about Layern, our brother, lets hear some excitement."

"Shit, I'm excited, brother. I always knew Layern would come back, which, by the way, will make his gift more intense. So hiding any feelings is not happening any more. But you said something I don't think I heard correctly; you had a human female tell you no to sex. So spill," Draken says. Shit, I don't want to have a talk about this. I have things under control.

"Draken, yes, I got a no from this woman, but I will have her. This is me, Showken. I always get what I want. She's playing hard to get right now, plus Layern says she has some issues, yet the predator in me is watching my prey, and soon I'll pounce." Draken is laughing so hard on the other end it's pissing me off. "Draken, stop laughing at me, you know I hate that shit!"

"Okay, brother, I'm sorry," Draken says, still chuckling. "Cess says I need to laugh more, and this was perfect for me to try out my new-found laughter." I never wanted to fuck Draken up until right now. "Listen, my brother," he says, and his voice becomes serious. "Be open to different."

"What the hell does that mean? Draken, go wake your Wella and tell her you're sick. Don't spout wisdom to me. You have not been married that long. I'll talk with you later," I say.

"Okay, talk later, and Showken?"

"What?"

"Good luck," he says, and the call goes dead. This is not funny. Marilyn, you have no idea what you just unleashed. I grab the keys and walk out of the door.

MARILYN

"Showken is driving me crazy. I mean, who does he think he is?" I say to Bruiser. He just looks at me. I've tried to watch a movie, and the house is spotless from all the cleaning I've done. Now I keep thinking about Showken. I feel like trash, knowing he just wants to fuck me. Yet, he did say he would be my friend . . . but that's bullshit. Showken just wants me to be his friend so I will let my guard down. I won't do it. I go to the kitchen and start making my dinner. I've not eaten this much since . . . gosh, I can't remember. Well, I had a big breakfast and a good lunch. I think I will keep the momentum up since it's my day off, stuffed chicken it is. I prepare everything, and find myself becoming more relaxed now that I've told Showken it's not going to happen, and he's way too busy to try to change my mind. I place the chicken in the oven, start peeling sweet potatoes for a side and get lost in the T.V. watching a reality show. I hear a knock on the door and thunder outside, all at the same time. I stare at the door, getting a warm feeling inside, knowing that it's him, maybe if I pretend I'm not here he will leave.

"Open the door, Marilyn, the food smells so good," Showken says. I bite my lip and stare at the door. Shit, this guy doesn't give up. The thunder strikes again, as I walk slowly to the door, stand next to it, then I hear the rain. I can't let him in.

"Go home, Showken," I say.

"No, Marilyn, open the door and let me eat some of your cooking, it smells really good," he says. "I know you are standing next to the door, unlock it, Marilyn, and invite me in."

I pull the door open, and before I can say anything, he's inside, placing a bottle of wine on my counter. This guy is unbelievable. He looks very nice in his sweaty t-shirt. I just look at him as he goes into my kitchen, opening cabinets and grabbing two glasses. I don't have any wine glasses; I'm not into things like that.

"Showken?"

"Marilyn, come have a drink with me." Showken says, not smiling, but giving me the sexiest look I've ever seen. Shit, he's here to seduce me.

I pick up the glass and take a very small sip, walking back to the kitchen, knife still in my hand. Pointing the knife at him, I say,

"You are taking a risk coming here at night. I could have fired a warning shot." He raises an eyebrow at me, but I'm trying to scare him some. Staring at his amazing green eyes, I blink a few times just to make sure this is not a dream. Who has eyes as beautiful as this?

"I'm never at risk, love, and I wanted to see you. So, I smell stuffed chicken and you're peeling sweet potatoes, what else is on the menu?" he asks, taking a drink, not removing his eyes from mine. I take a deep breath, and decide just dinner won't be so bad.

"That's dinner, and dessert will be the cupcakes I picked up from Wal-Mart. I know you are probably used to fancy meals, but this is as fancy as it gets," I say, turning away from him as I finish cutting up the sweet potatoes. How could he want a waitress at a bar and a cashier at a gas station? He's some rich billionaire, and he chooses to have dinner with me in a one bedroom apartment. I don't get it. "Why are you here, Showken?" I snap at him.

"I missed your company, and I like being around you." he says, as if he's telling himself new information. "I haven't figured it out, yet I feel like I should be around you. I don't- can I stay and have dinner with you, please?" he asks. I turn and finish chopping the sweet potatoes, placing them in a pot to boil. I turn and look him up and down, enjoying his body.

"You are here now, you can stay for dinner, nothing else," I specify, avoiding any eye contact.

"Thanks, I'm going to get comfortable," he says, pulling off his t-shirt. I almost reach out to touch his chest. Shit, I think fainting is a strong possibility with his shirt off. Oh my, I knew he had a great body, but he is built everywhere. He also has this badass tattoo on his chest and arm. I so want to lick them. Oh shit, I don't know where these feelings are coming from for this man. The rain starts hitting the window, near the patio door. He turns and looks at me, and my mouth is getting really dry. "You okay? You look different," he says, catching my eye, and everything south is running into my panties now. He starts to walk towards me and it's like I'm in a trance, I can't move. He leans down and gives my lips a slow lick from corner to corner, and he pulls back.

"Just as I thought, a slice of heaven," he says, looking like a very aroused man now. "How long before dinner?" he asks, stepping back. Instantly I want his touch again.

"Umm, it should be ready in about an hour," I say, knowing my face is red from that very hot sexy thing he just did with my lips. You would think I could contain my emotions, and usually I can, but Showken is breaking down my walls quickly.

"Great, I can't wait to *eat*," he says, with an emphasis on 'eat'. I can't help but think he is talking about more than food, and I'm sure I want him more than food right now. I grab my glass and take a huge gulp of this fantastic wine he's brought. He watches me move around the kitchen as I make up Bruiser's food. He doesn't say a word. I feel like he is talking, but with his eyes; they are following me, and my body is yearning now. He finally breaks the silence.

"You have siblings?" he asks.

"Uhh, no. It's just me," I say, really not wanting to talk about myself. "Do you have brothers or sisters?" I ask, giving him the same question to see how he likes the hot seat.

"Yes, there are ten of us altogether, nine boys and one girl," Showken says, with a smirk. I wonder what that is about.

"Wow, your mother must really like kids. I couldn't imagine having that many kids," I say, taking out the butter and brown sugar for the sweet potatoes. I can't wait to eat.

"Well, we have big families, and it's kind of a tradition. Anything under seven is unheard of. How many kids do you want?"

I look up at him as if he's confessed a murder.

"I will never have kids, ever," I say, turning away from him and feeling tears building up in my eyes. I feel him standing behind me and I can't move or speak. I turn and he pulls me into his arms, and the tears are pouring down. I'm a product of bad blood; I won't take the risk of bringing a child into this world, knowing where it comes from. I wipe my tears and turn to finish dinner. We don't speak again until I'm pulling the cupcakes out of the fridge.

"Showken, do you want a cupcake or two," I say, as he has eaten everything already. After I fixed my plate and told him to eat as much as he wanted, he finished the other three stuffed chicken breasts and all of the potatoes. I couldn't get upset, because he ate in silence and seemed to enjoy every bite.

"Yes, I'll have one," he says, moving to the sofa in front of the television. I see Bruiser is stuffed as he lies on his side, watching. I walk over and hand him a double chocolate cupcake; he sets it down on the table in front of him. I glance over and look at his chest, again. He has the best body ever.

"Showken, you don't like chocolate?" I ask peeling down my cupcake paper. I take a bite, and see him watching me, licking his lips.

"Yes, I love chocolate, but I'll wait to eat mine. You enjoy," he says, and his eyes roam my body. I can't eat with him watching me like this. I take one more bite, and set it down. I stand and his hand touches my knee, oh, my body is way too responsive to him. I look up and he is smiling.

"Wait, I want to eat my dessert now." He gives a wicked smile, and I think my eyes will come out of my head. I've never had a guy so smooth. "Don't I get to eat my dessert, Marilyn?" he asks, but I'm not sure why he's asking. I know he's speaking of something else. I'm 27 years old and I know when I see a horny man. He turns with one leg bent and the other on the floor as he faces me. I turn slowly to see him, and his sweat pants are hanging slightly from his waist. My body feels shaky inside.

"Umm, Showken?"

"No, can I eat my dessert is the question I asked, and I want only a yes or no answer," he says, and I'm pretty sure a growl comes from him. That is not possible, he cannot growl. I glance at Bruiser and he's sleeping, shit. What a great guard dog, sleeping on the job. We stare at each other and he's not backing down, I'm not either. We just stare at each other. I think he will give up, but he doesn't. After about five minutes, I give in.

"Yes, you can." He spins me around on the sofa and pulls my pants down so fast I'm blinking uncontrollably.

"Thank you." He grabs the cupcake and begins pushing up my shirt, smearing the frosting over my abdomen, sliding my panties down with his other hand he continues to smear frosting on my inner hips, moving towards my sex. When all of the frosting is gone, he stuffs the cupcake in his mouth and barely chews and swallows.

"I like to eat my frosting last," he says, lowering his head. He starts licking me in long strokes, licking the chocolate off me. I should push him away. I should say no, but damn, it feels way too good to stop. I'm glad I shaved my privates, I'm sure frosting and hair don't mix. He didn't know that, though, maybe he's a freak. I'm brought out of my thoughts fast, as each lick becomes hot to my body, literally. I can feel heat. It feels good, though, and a moan escapes my mouth, "Ahhh, Mmmm," I hear and can't believe I'm doing this. He spreads my legs farther apart, holding them up.

"You are so delicious, Marilyn," he says, going straight to my sex. Opening my folds with his tongue, he sucks and pulls on me. This is so crazy, I can't believe myself. When I feel his tongue go inside me I scream, "AHHHHHHHHH!" He must like that, because he continues to hold my legs apart and his tongue is going in . . . out . . . in . . . out. I feel my head shaking, going back and forth. I need to get away from him. I try to move, and his hands grip my legs.

"Marilyn, let go for me, I want all of my dessert." That is enough for me and I begin to come. He holds his mouth to me, sucking, making sure he draws out my orgasm. He continues to kiss my inner thighs, sucking and biting me. He moves his body up mine and places my legs around his waist. He pushes up my bra and starts sucking my nipples, hard. They instantly harden, and I can't believe that I'm allowing this. He comes to my ear.

"Marilyn, you are so beautiful and sweet, and I want you," he says, as he starts to grind his sex on me with his sweats on. I can't, this is so wrong, how did I get into this. "Marilyn, stop thinking and let me, please," he says, as he stares into my eyes waiting for an answer. He is still moving, and I just nod a yes. He stands, pulling me with him, and he is in my bedroom fast. He never lets me go; gripping my ass he lowers me to the bed and kisses my ear, my neck, and my shoulders. I feel him pushing his pants down, and now I feel his sex on mine and he's so hard and huge. Wait, he has to put on a condom.

"Showken, condoms, in my drawer," I say, panting.

"I'm okay, I don't need one," he says, sliding in a finger, and I respond so well. He slides it in . . . out . . . in . . . out, and instead of just putting in another finger he pushes in two more. Shit, that hurts.

"Showken, that hurts," I say, and he moves down my body, not saying a word, and pulls my clitoris with his mouth, as he

37

continues to push his fingers inside of me. It no longer hurts, but I can feel him stretching me out, crossing the fingers like scissors inside of me.

"Just relax, I'm going to get you ready for me," he says, coming back up my body, taking in my breast and sucking it hard again. I feel my body preparing for another orgasm.

"Yes, Marilyn, another one. Let me feel you come on my fingers, now." Again I release, and my body is going crazy. He pulls his fingers out and licks each finger that I've exploded on. I don't know why, but that turns me on something bad. He still hasn't gone for a condom.

"Showken, you have to put on a condom, we have to be safe," I say, panting, not wanting to get pregnant or catch an STD.

"I'm clean, and even if you're not, it won't affect me," he says, placing his sex right at my entrance. I don't know why I believe him, or maybe it's just so intense. I can't stop myself, and with his eyes closed he pushes himself inside me and shit, this is hurting. I don't say anything, knowing my body will adjust. He doesn't move, and starts a very deep kiss with me. Our tongues dance, and he licks my lips and sucks them in between kisses. I feel my body warming and I push towards him. I feel the smile on my face and he begins to thrust, in . . . out . . . in . . . out. He continues to move slowly. My body wants more and I start moving faster and he stops, letting me catch my breath he starts again this time grabbing my hips, moving me to his speed. He goes slow, then fast, and then slow again. I try not to scream, but he gives a good push and I'm screaming, "IT FEEELS SOOOO GOOOD!!" And he does it again.

"You feel amazing, I want to stay like this, beautiful," he says. I wrap my arms around his neck and try to push him over, and it's like trying to move a building. He's solid. He smiles and rolls over to his back, holding me tight, never pulling out of me. I can't move, oh my, he's so big, I think he's touching too many of my insides. He starts to move, and I close my eyes and just feel. I start to move up and down and he's guiding me. I place my hands on his chest and really start to move, I feel him squeezing my breast and my juices are running out of me, making it easier to move. Throwing back my head I feel the heat building inside of me, my body is on fire for this man. For the first time I hear him moan, "Mmmm, yes sweetness!" Those words are comforting, even though he knows I don't like terms of endearment, he keeps calling me by those terms. I'm sure on purpose.

"Showken," I say, as he grasps my hips and pushes in deep. He sits up and I wrap my arms around him, meeting each thrust with my body.

"Let me feel you come around me again, baby," he says, and I try to hold out and I'm pulling at his hair and my body has a mind of its own as I try to escape his arms. This orgasm is just too much. I want this, and yet I'm trying to run away from it at the same time. I finally relax and his arms loosen and I'm panting like Bruiser. I was not supposed to sleep with this man. Shit, we didn't use a condom.

"Stop thinking, Marilyn, and just relax after sex," he says, turning to lay me down and gently pulling out of me. I thought he was going to get up. He positions himself behind me, pulling me close. I feel sleep coming, and just as I'm closing my eyes I think I heard him say, "My Marilyn". I smile at the thought, and sleep overtakes me.

SHOWKEN

What the hell am I doing? I should not be cuddling her, yet I can't bring myself to move. She felt so good exploding for me that I can still feel her. I'm usually a one-night type of guy, but Marilyn makes me want a few more nights with her. She's an awesome lover. Shit, did I just think lover? Those beautiful grey eyes are amazing. I take a peek at her sleeping, and she looks so soft, which I know is not the truth. She has some deep feelings against her family, and I need to find out what they are. I smell Bruiser enter the room, and see him sit at the door. I reach my hand out for him. He comes to me, and I rub his head. He recognizes the beast in me, and knows I'm more than man. Luckily, he can't speak. I look him in the eyes and send him a good feeling. He barks loudly, and before I'm aware of it, I'm laughing out loud. I feel Marilyn stirring, and turn to give her a morning kiss. I know she's sore, I'm going to have to run her a bath, I didn't mean to work her over like that, but that first taste was too good.

"Good morning, sexy," I say. When she told me not to call her by terms of endearment, it became my duty to do so.

"Good morning, and I see you keep using sweet words for me still," she says, with slight smile.

"Well, you are so beautiful, precious. I just can't help myself, honey," I say, chuckling. I feel her hand on my chest, rubbing my birthmark, which humans always think is a tattoo. My beast responds and growls inside me. She has to stop that, or I'll be inside her again. I grab her hand and start sucking her fingers. I send heat into each one, giving her a little fire to distract her. She moans, "Ahhh." I smile and go in for a kiss, I know I have shocked her because she is hesitant, but she gives in.

"I have to get ready for work, I have to be at my first job at 10 a.m.," she says. I don't want her to go to work. I am even more concerned that she says her first job. Shit, how many jobs does she have?

"Marilyn, what are your dreams?" I ask. I would like to know if she's happy. I shouldn't care, usually I'm gone before they awaken, not even worrying about their soreness, but I feel something else with her. I like her smart mouth.

"What? Showken, I don't dream about anything anymore. Dreams don't come true."

"Yes they do, and I want to know what is the one thing you

would like to do?" I ask, turning her on her back and positioning myself to hover over her delicious body. Those curves; she is truly awesome, and I want to feel them, after she tells me her dream.

"Showken, you are not listening, I really don't know. I used to dream, but that was a long time ago," she says, looking away from my face. She's lying; she knows what she wants. I quickly grab her legs and hold them up in the air. I hear her gasp.

"Showken, what are you doing? I need to go take a shower and get ready for work," she says, but I smell her arousal rising.

"First, a shower is not going to help, and second, you should know I don't like to be lied to. So try again, dream . . . " I say, tilting my head as I push the tip of my sex inside her.

"Showken, mmm. I can't think like this," she says, trying to pull away. I like this; she's a ton of fun. I pull out and do it again. "SHOWKEN!" she yells, and I like the sound of that.

"Dream, gorgeous," I say, smiling. She is getting frustrated.

"I wanted to be a painter, satisfied?" she says, and I thrust all the way into her.

"Yes I am," I say, giving her a proper morning wake-up. When we finish, I know for sure I'm going to have to put her in the tub, but she thinks she's just going to walk into the bathroom. She pulls back the covers and sits up.

"What are you doing? Stay here, I'll start the bath," I say, standing and heading for the bathroom. I look in and shit, it's tiny.

"I don't have time for a bath, I'll take a shower so I can get going," she says, and I start laughing. She's so determined.

"I think you should stay right there and wait for me," I say, turning and starting the bath water. I blow into the water, and hopefully my fire can take her soreness away. I come back into the room, only to find Marilyn lying on the floor and Bruiser licking her face. She looks pissed. I chuckle, for one I didn't hear her fall, and second she looks adorable on the floor naked with Bruiser licking her face.

"Stop your smirking and help me up, please," she snaps. I walk over and stand there, shaking my head. I told this stubborn woman to be still.

"I told you to wait for me," I say, trying to contain my laughter, but I can't. I'm in full hysterics in no time.

"This is not funny, Showken, you did this on purpose," she says, in full pout mode.

"Yes, I did do it on purpose. I wanted you to feel so good, and by the looks of it you forgot I held your legs up for hours. Bruiser, stop licking her face," I say, bending and picking her up. I walk her into the bathroom and gently lower her into the tub.

"Showken, I need to get ready, and, umm, you don't have to stay. In fact, I can't think straight, and really need time alone," she says, looking me in the eye. Those grey eyes are so fucking beautiful. I shouldn't care that she wants me to leave, I'm usually the one leaving anyway, but I don't want to leave right now. I will respect her wish, though, this time.

"Oh, yeah, I need to get home and start getting prepared for work tomorrow," I say, feeling strange. I don't like this feeling. I turn and walk into the bedroom, slipping my clothes back on, giving Bruiser a rub and heading for her door.

"Hurry up so you can come lock your door, love," I say, shutting the door, not wanting to hear her complaining about taking care of herself. I drive myself home and walk into my room, crashing on the bed. I need to rest before work tomorrow.

***

Walking into work with my brothers and not having Draken here is strange. He has always made sure everything went along fine with the business. I pass my secretary going to my office. I don't want Draken's office, he may show up at any time. He's very controlling, but I would kill for my brother.

"Mr. Draglen," Kim says, as I turn my doorknob. I turn and see the woman smiling at me. She's very attractive, and any other time I would be flirting with her, but I can't get my mind off Marilyn.

"Showken, remember? I'm not my brother, just Showken," I say, giving her a small smile and causing her to blush furiously. Shit. I can't flirt with you, lady. Let me get into my office.

"Okay, Showken. Your 10 a.m. is on the phone and would like to do a conference call with you right now. What would you like to do?" she asks, falling back into business mode.

"Really? Okay, tell him I'll be ready in five minutes, and then just transfer the call. Let my brothers know that I'm doing a conference call with the banks and if at least one could join. That will be great," I say, walking away and shutting my door. Today is a big day, as three large banking corporations are approaching us with investments to help insure our funding. This will be a lucrative deal for the family, to increase our wealth in this land. I can't screw this up, but I'm missing Marilyn's touch and her snappy mouth. I had better be focused on this deal, or Draken will come visit, and everyone knows he's a hard ass. I'm pulled out of my thoughts when the phone rings, Kim's voice comes in.

"Mr. Showken, Domlen has agreed to join you on the call; shall I connect you now?" she says, and I'm amazed at how she still puts Mr. in front of Showken.

"Yes, Kim, thanks," I say, and I'm connected with the conference call in seconds. Everyone does greetings, and I start off by saying, "Out of World Enterprises will expect nothing less than what we offer on every fifty million we supply or insure." I'm glad Domlen is on this call, he's a hard ass, too, and doesn't negotiate. He's offer or no offer. The meeting lasts over forty-five minutes, but in the end Draglen brothers are able to close the deal. I feel very proud right now, and would like to share the good news with someone. My mind instantly goes to Marilyn, and I think maybe I should send a text. I don't want to bother her at work with a ringing cell. Shit, I need to get a grip, but after my text.

Hey, beautiful. Hope work is going well for you. I just wanted to share that I closed a really big deal today and yeah just want to share with someone. Showken

Draglen.

I hope she responds. I begin typing on another project we are working on with some of the oil companies. My cell beeps, I shouldn't be excited, but I am.

Hello Showken, glad you closed a deal. Umm I really don't know anything about this deal, but I'm still happy for you. Marilyn.

She responded, shit. I'm not sure what to do. I never see a woman for more than one night, but with her I need to see her again, tonight. I can't be falling for her, I think the smart mouth and the hot sex has me wanting more. Well, I've had some very hot sex with some women, but I never texted them the next day. Marilyn, I need to figure out your pull on me. I text back:

So, when you get off tonight can I see you again? Showken Draglen.

I can't believe I just texted that. I sound desperate. I should just walk away. I've already had sex with her, if I stick around she'll become needy. I'm not ready to settle down. My phone beeps and I grab it fast. She truly excites me.

Showken, we had a good time last night and I think it would be best if we leave it just like that. I don't and really am not ready to start seeing anyone. I enjoyed you last night, but we can't see each other again. Take care. Marilyn.

Fuck, she just shut me down after a night of hot sex? I've never had this happen. My beast is pissed. I look at my reflection in the glass of the picture of my siblings on my desk, and, sure enough, my eyes are glowing. I will the door to lock, just in case my brothers want to come in. I can't believe she said take care, what kind of shit is that? Fuck that. I text back:

We need to discuss this in person and take care Marilyn, don't piss me off. Showken Draglen.

I'm pacing my office right now. If there is going to be anyone getting let go it's her, not me. She's trying to shut me down again. My cell beeps.

Showken I don't owe you shit and if I say it's over then it's over just accept it and move on please and stop texting me. Marilyn.

WHAT! I should just accept it and leave her alone, but not when she says so. Marilyn, you pissed off a dragon and you don't even know it.

Precious, you have no idea who you're trying to shut down. I don't do shut down and you have caused me a very stressful day now. I WILL SEE YOU LATER! Showken Draglen.

I don't know who she thinks she is. I do the break-ups, not her. I say when, and I'm not done. My phone rings and I snatch it and scream "Hello" forgetting I'm at work.

"Showken, I see you're really pissed and it has to do with Marilyn. I told you to leave her alone."

"Layern, this is not the fucking time. You know you should not get into this, I know to leave her alone, but when I'm done with her!" I snap.

"You're joking right, listen, the longer you stay around this woman the more attached you will be, and I know all about being attached, but if you want her then go for her, just don't pretend you don't want her."

"Pretending, I'm not fucking pretending," I growl. I can't believe she got me like this. I look and she's not responded yet, this is not happening. I'm her one night stand, NO! I will not allow it.

"Brother, calm down." Layern says, forcefully. "You know what your beast can do. Get it together and let her go. I'm sure your eyes are glowing, and you know your beast has issues with rejection, get calm now," I know this is to calm my beast and bring me back from anger. My beast can get angry, and once it's angry, a true beast rises. Marilyn started this and damn it, she will not end it.

"I'm calm, I need to get off the phone," I say, hanging up the phone and sending another text:

Beautiful, I know my last text was demanding and really I'm not that guy. I just need to understand how you can shut off something that you know we have together, I'm sorry for using caps, which I know means yelling. I'm angry at me. I want to see you and I know you do too, I'm not sure why you are denying yourself. Please forgive me and speak with me. Showken Draglen.

I fumble around my desk waiting for my phone to beep, and it seems like forever, but it does.

First my name is Marilyn get that in your head and second. Why can't you respect my decision? You should not make this hard. We had fun. I enjoyed you Showken, but like I said I never wanted this between us to happen, you seduced me. I'm not blaming you, but I didn't ask for this in fact you chased me down. It was only one night; please move on and yes I accept your apology. Now, I'm at work. Marilyn.

She's been sent into my life to put me through hell. There is no other way to explain this. I've never been rejected. If she wants to end then so be it, but I can make her wish she didn't. I will see her tonight, just not how she may have thought.

Marilyn, I understand. Showken Draglen.

After I hit send, I call up an old friend of mine to see about a night at a bar. Narrowing my eyes, I feel my beast pacing inside and I calm him. It's not long before everything's set for tonight. I have a surprise for Marilyn, and she'll confess her real feelings, and then I will be able to let her go. I first need to do a background check on her; her crying about her family makes me wonder if this could be a reason for her bitterness. What is in her past that has her closed? This is a job for Hawken. I close my eyes, pushing on my brother's mind, and I feel him try to pull away, that makes me chuckle. He finally lets me in, and I tell him I need all information on Marilyn Carrington. He agrees reluctantly, but I know he can get it done with his brilliant computer skills. I start to feel better about Marilyn; she's not going to be able to resist me. I feel the cell from my real home ringing. Shit, it's Mother.

"Hello, Mother," I say, not greeting her as I would in our land.

"My son," Mother says. "I see a woman, and I think you like her. I warn you though, she's not like other women you're used to." Her gift for her children is amazing; she always sees things when we don't want her to. Layern gets his gift from her, and although she says his is stronger, I have yet to see him predict like her.

"Do not worry, Mother. I promise my affairs with that woman are temporary. I'm here on business and just like to have fun," I say, hoping she will leave this subject alone.

"My son, your brother Draken did not listen, and you see he is married now. So, because I know how you and your beast are, I need to stay closer to you, as you and your beast tend to lose control. I will keep more of a close eye on you. Remember, your beast is the powerful green; you have not taken a Wella, which would have helped you, my son. Now, what is the human's name?"

"Marilyn," I say, feeling like a fucking kid. I hate when she's right, and I hate it even more when I can't say anything back. My mother can be really sweet, but she's the deadliest beast I know. It's best to agree and not anger her.

"Marilyn, what a very sophisticated name. My son, I will speak with you later," she says, and the phone is dead. I'm not sure what the hell is private in this family. My brother can sense your feelings and my mother can see your future, not to mention my other brothers have gifts, fuck. I hear knocking and I will the door unlocked. Hawken comes strolling in like he's a model.

"Hey, you got the information?" I ask, rubbing my hands in my hair.

"Yes, I do. Showken, this is not the type of woman you usually deal with. I mean just look," Hawken says, handing me a stack of papers, shit, this is not a good sign.

I begin to read them.

Marilyn Jackie Carrington born December 20th 1986

Mother- Linda Mary Boren

Father-John Steve Carrington

Marilyn Carrington was removed from her mother's care at 9 years old after suffering a sexual assault by her mother's boyfriend Richard Thomas. Linda Boren refused to remove the boyfriend and Marilyn was never reunited with her mother. Marilyn was placed in her father's care until the age of 16 years old, when she petitioned the court to be emancipated. No reason was given and John Carrington didn't contest this.

"Shit, Hawken, I wasn't expecting this. What kind of parents did Marilyn have? I don't think I need to read any more," I say, turning the stack over. Damn. She carries a gun, has a guard dog and wants to be left alone. I'm guessing she has never been able to trust anyone.

"Showken, I think you should leave her alone. She's not what you want to deal with, and look at you digging up information and shit on this girl. Let her go," Hawken says, giving me a serious look. This is a lot to take in, but I can't let her go now, that is what she's expecting, but I will teach her a lesson today.

"Hawken, thanks for the information and advice, but I have my own plans, and leaving her alone is not on the list," I say. A growl escapes my mouth.

"Oh, I see," Hawken says, rising. "Showken, I'm just worried. Be careful, and get her out of your system," he says heading out the door. I sit there thinking about tonight, and how I can play this out without fucking up my chance. I decide to leave right after 2 p.m. I can do the rest of my calls at home. I walk past Kim, and don't realize I didn't say anything until I'm in my car driving home.

MARILYN

I wish Showken had never come over last night. I hope he takes the hint and realizes he and I can't be a 'we'. Last night was the first time I had ever let myself go with a man. I'm usually very guarded. I don't feel like going to the bar tonight, but I need the money. I've been saving for a newer car. I pull into the parking lot and sit for a few minutes before my shift starts. It's a nice crowd, but nothing like the weekends, this is the after work crowd. I hear my phone ringing and it's Jasmine.

"Hello," I say.

"Don't hello me, you usually call me on your day off, and this has been our ritual for two years. So what happened last night?

Any nightmares?" Jasmine asks, sounding really concerned. I hate when I have nightmares, but last night was a fantasy. I wish I could be in a relationship, but I don't want to bring my baggage to Showken. He would run for the hills.

"Marilyn? Huh? What you thinking about?" Jasmine asks.

I sigh, I know telling her will only ease her mind. I take a deep breath and let it spill.

"I fucked Showken last night," I say, waiting for it. There is silence and then a lot of screaming and laughing.

"Holy fuckballs Batman! Bitch, you were digging him, I knew it. All of that talk and he got to you. Is he good? I bet he's awesome in bed with that body and those eyes . . . shit, I wish I were you. Damn. You finally got some,"

"Jazz, yes it was awesome, yes it's the best I've ever had and I couldn't fucking walk, but," I say hesitating.

"No buts, you deserves this. Please Mari, tell me you didn't give him the boot?" she pleads. I climb out of the car and head towards the back door to start my shift. I'm glad we close early tonight.

"Mari listen, he's what you need to find your way back into the world of dating, and who knows, you might fall for him," she says. I walk into the bar and head towards the front. I'm still talking on the phone when I see him. He has his arm around some whore and is having a beer with her. I hear Jasmine calling my name. I'm fucking shocked; he was just begging to see me tonight. The tears are filling my eyes, and I refuse to let one drop. He looks up and makes eye contact with me, and we stare at each other. Fuck him, I say to myself, turning to head back out the door. I can't do this today, not now. He used me like everyone does. Hanging up the cell phone, I make a dash for my car. I hear running behind me, and turning around I see Showken, right there spinning me around. Reflex kicks in and I begin to fight. I'm crying uncontrollably while I'm kicking and punching him.

"Marilyn, please just listen, it's not what you think," he says.

"Fuck you; get your hands off me before I yell rape!" He stares at me strangely. I can't even be sorry for saying that right now. He used me and just wanted to get into my pants, just like I thought. "LET ME GO NOW!" I yell. He finally releases me and I make my way to my car. I'll call in a few minutes and inform my boss I'm not coming in. Showken follows.

"Marilyn please, I just was trying to get you to see me tonight, I wasn't thinking, I don't want that girl, I want you. I ran after you, please don't shut me out, please, please, I'm so sorry," he says, and I see a flicker in his eyes, but I shake my head. I can't do this. People always hurt me. My cell phone starts ringing and it's Jasmine. I hit ignore. Climbing into my car, I start the engine and drive off.

I don't know where I'm going, but I can't go home, he will only follow me there. I just drive. I call my boss to let him know I need a few days off; he agrees, and I fill up my tank and drive. Showken used me. I can't believe I fell for him. I don't have anywhere to go. I can't go to Jasmine's, because he might know where she stays. I feel the tears come again. I'm so stupid for allowing this to happen to me, again. Nobody wants me; I will always be an unloved woman. Why would he want me, my own mother didn't want me, she chose her loser boyfriend over me. My father is no better, he was all good until my body started developing, but then when the money was low, he used me to pay the bills by selling my body to his friends. I'm everyone's girl to use.

All my boyfriends throughout my life have always used me for something. I drive to where I can become invisible, Samuel's place. I pull into the driveway and I'm greeted by Mona, Samuel's 'man girl'. I will lie low here for a day. Nobody knows I sold myself for a few years in my teens. Samuel won't ask for anything except money, and I will give him two hundred bucks and that will take care of a one-day stay. I go in and make the deal with Samuel, and I go to a room that is mine for the night.

I walk in and go sit in the chair by the window and cry. I cry for believing that someone could actually want me, the fact is I'm only good for being used. My phone begins to ring and I see it's Showken. I hit ignore and get a voice message. It rings again and the same thing happens. This continues for the next five hours, Showken calling, I hit ignore and he leaves a message. I should turn my phone off, but I can't in this house. I never know if Samuel is in trouble, and I need to let someone know where to find me. I finally call Jasmine.

"Marilyn, I've been worried sick about you, where are you?

Showken called me and told me what happened. Oh honey, I'm so sorry. You can believe I asked him if he decided to eat some Dicko cereal this morning," Jasmine says, and I smile, imagining Jasmine going off on Showken, I'm sure he didn't get a word in.

"I'm fine, just need to clear my head, you know. I mean, Jazz, everyone uses me, except for you of course. But I'm just a toy to people, to use whenever they choose," I say, not realizing the tears are flowing again. My door opens and a woman peers in, she pulls her client out to go into another room.

"Fuck him Mari, you are beautiful, smart and my best friend. I love you. Please don't run, just come over, I already have Bruiser, I went to your house and you weren't there. I'm worried."

"I know, umm I will come over tomorrow. I promise, I just need tonight to get my head on straight, I need to go," I say, feeling a full crying spell coming on, again.

"Okay, Mari, but your behind needs to be at my house tomorrow morning or I'm reporting you missing," Jasmine says. I know she's serious, and I will be at her house tomorrow, I just need to feel this pain.

"Okay, bye."

"Bye, Mari. Tomorrow morning or missing persons' report," she says. I hang up, and look out the window at the busy traffic outside the house. Samuel always keeps you working seven days a week. I look at my phone and I have twenty messages from Showken. Why is he doing this? He got what he wanted. I get out my gun, placing it beside my thigh away from the door, this will keep me safe for tonight, but tomorrow I will be gone. I go into my shell and look at the men and women coming and going from Samuel's place.

***

The next morning I say my goodbyes to Samuel, he tells me I'm always welcome and I leave without any problems. Samuel may have used me in the past, selling me for money, but it was my choice. I made the decision to stay, and I made the decision to leave. My mind is clear and I'm not crying any more. I will not be used any longer. Showken doesn't exist to me any longer. He's dead to me, like my father and mother.

SHOWKEN

"LAYERN I NEED TO FIND HER NOOOOOW!!" I yell, trying to gain some composure. I can't believe myself. I'm a fool. The look in her eyes is nothing but hurt.

"Showken, calm down. If I do find her, you can't go see her like this. You need to calm down," Layern says, calmly. He is such an ass.

"FUCK CALM!" I yell, picking up the sofa in the living area and throwing it into the kitchen. I can't find her because she's hiding from me. I have been calling, texting, and I even talked with Jasmine, who called me names I never heard of. I deserve it, though. I've never felt so bad in my life. How could I do this to her?

"Showken, you need to get control, and stop throwing furniture," Domlen says, narrowing his eyes. I take a deep breath, and my beast calms.

"Domlen, I hurt her bad. I saw it in her eyes. I don't know what to do, I can't leave her alone, I have to fix this. I have to." I continue to pace, and I look over and notice that my brother, who is always talking, is now quiet. He knows something.

"Hawken, do you know where she might be? I looked through those papers and went to every street address on them, using my powers, and I didn't find her," I snap, balling my fists. I'm really trying to keep my monster inside.

"Look at you, Showken, you are in no condition to see her, especially when your beast is itching to come out." He knows, but doesn't want to tell me. I know how my beast can get, but if I just see her and know she is okay. I will calm down.

"Hawken, I'm only going to ask you this once. Do you know where Marilyn is?" I ask, barely raising my voice. There is silence in the room. I look in Hawken's eyes and know that he has information on where she might be. I growl, and I feel my beast coming out. I shoot fire at Hawken as he makes a run, and his beast becomes angry.

"GIVE ME THE ADDRESS!" I yell, and my voice is rough and raspy. I'm changing. Shit.

"Showken, just breathe," Layern says, holding his hands up. I'm looking at Hawken, waiting for the address, when Mother comes through her portal, extremely fast. What the fuck!

"Showken, you are coming home," she says. She reaches out and grabs me by my throat, she opens another portal and pulls me through. I can't fucking believe this shit. We end up in the garden and I notice then, I'm in my full dragon now, damn. I can't talk, and I hear the roaring coming from me.

"Showken, you are out of control. You need to just get calm, I've revoked your portal until I believe that you will not expose or kill a son of mine," she says, walking over to a table. She glares and I growl out in anger, knowing she holds the control. My dragon whimpers. I see Draken and Cess walking up. I can hear them talking.

"Oh Draken, he is just lying there. I feel so bad for him," Cess says. My mother turns back to me and begins to rub my head, and tears start rolling down my face. I hate that my dragon gets out of control. It's now got in the way of me making it right with Marilyn. Mother will never let me leave unless she feels I'm okay.

"Princess, I know Showken's dragon can get out of control sometimes. It's best to let our mother calm him," Draken says, and I see the look in his eyes. Draken always came to my rescue growing up, when my brothers would pick on me. I want to speak, yet all that comes out is a growl.

"I'm going over there," Cess says, and tries to pass Draken. He pulls her into his arms.

"Princess, where do you think you're going?"

"Over there with Showken, he's my brother and friend,

62

Draken. I want to see if I can help."

"I say you can't help. Besides, you know how my dragon and I feel about touching." Draken raises a brow at Cess. She smiles, and I wish Marilyn would smile at me like that. I need to get back.

"Draken, please, you know it's always just you, don't be jealous."

I see Draken look at me and I close my eyes. I need to calm myself to shift so I can talk.

"Okay, but we do it my way," Draken says.

"What way is that?" Cess says. I feel my brother's presence, and feel his hand on my side. My breathing is fast. I know I'm very dangerous like this. I don't blame Draken for protecting Cess from me. I can't hurt another.

"Come, Princess, and place your hand on mine, he will feel your touch, not mine." She looks skeptical for a few seconds, but does as he asks. Cess' touch is comforting; she truly cares for me. I growl again, and I feel Draken lift his hand a little. I whimper, informing him that I don't want this. This is how I get my dragon under control. After a while Draken and Cess leave, but mother never does. She orders everyone out of the garden and begins to talk.

"Showken, well you have always been so much like me. I, too, could not control my beast at one time. You are not alone. This human has touched my son, the son who vowed not to marry for at least another hundred years," she says, leaning to kiss my horn. "My son, of all my Youngs you are the one I worry most about. I know things, my son."

I growl, not wanting to talk, I need to get back to Marilyn.

"Shhh, listen, I know you are feeling things that are foreign to you, but I know the problem, you love her."

I snuff, trying to blow that thought off.

"Showken, you are in love, I know because this is how I reacted to your father. I am you and you are me, do you understand? Yes, of course you do. This human is truly guarded, and I don't know what the future holds for you, but I will tell you this, this human can be the remedy to this struggle with your beast. Your father is mine, and she will be yours, I think. I will send you back once you can shift and I see that you have yourself under control. I love you, my son, you are just like me, embrace your beast, love and you will gain freedom," she says, continuing to rub my head. I finally drift off to sleep, knowing I've hurt Marilyn.

***

The next morning, I'm in my bed in the castle. I climb out of bed, running both hands through my hair. I stretch, feeling better. I walk over to my table and see a tray of fruit and cheese with a cup of tea. Beauka is one crazy dragon. I eat the tray of food and go take a shower. After my shower, I slip on a pair of loose green slacks, walking out the door to find my mother. I need to get home and fix things with Marilyn. I find my mother in the flowers, walking and singing.

"My son, you are awake, finally, I've been waiting for you, don't do any formal hello, I know how you like them," she says, turning to look at me. This is her sarcasm.

"Thank you, mother, I would like to go back," I say, swallowing hard. I really need to check on Marilyn.

"You know I already knew you would want to go back. I will open the portal for you, but you must convince her to come see me," she says, leaning down, smiling at her flowers and walking closer to me. How the hell is that going to happen? I can't take her through the portal. My mother doesn't like coming to Earth, so I can only assume she means bring her here, but why?

"Mother, why do you want to meet her? And how do I set this up?" I ask, looking at her smile.

"Showken, use your gift and arrange a meeting, I want to meet her very soon, please don't keep me waiting," she says, waving her hand and opening a portal, yes. I didn't expect her to let me leave so soon, but I'm glad.

"Thank you Mother, I will set it up," I say, making a run for the portal, I can't wait to find Marilyn. I walk right into my room. I quickly dress and walk out my door. Hawken is standing with his arms folded.

"Feel better?" he asks.

"Yes, where is she?" I say, narrowing my eyes.

"She's at her friend's place, now."

"Now? Where she was at first?" I ask, worrying she's been with a man.

"Brother, just go to her friend's, it doesn't matter anyway. Layern says she's pretty hurt." Hawken confirms my fears. I walk past him, grabbing the keys to my Hummer and walking the door.

Driving to Jasmine's place, I can't help but think about how to fix this. I stop and grab some cupcakes. Finally making it to the apartment complex, I see Marilyn's car, she tries to hide. I step out of the car and sniff. Yes, she's here alright, she's trying to hide from me. I walk up to Jasmine's door and start knocking. I listen and can hear Bruiser barking, she's trying to quiet him. I keep knocking; I'm not leaving. The door swings open and Marilyn is standing in front of me, pointing a gun. This should be interesting. I walk past her and stroll in.

"Get out my house, you sorry piece of shit!" Jasmine yells.

"I will, once I make Marilyn understand I never meant to hurt her," I say, looking at Marilyn. She is still pointing the gun at me, not speaking. Bruiser comes up to me, I bend and give him a rub.

"Marilyn, please put that away, you could hurt someone," I say to her.

"I plan on hurting someone, now leave or I'll shoot you for breaking into my friend's house," she says, with a blank look. She means it, too. I need to get control, but not scare her.

"I see, you want me dead?" I say, looking at her. She looks amazing, and I just want to hug her and kiss her all over, but I must wait.

"Yes, she does want you dead, and so do I. Mari, go ahead, I didn't invite-" I interrupt her friend. Damn, she talks too much.

"Would you please leave us alone?" I ask, not taking my eyes off Marilyn.

"Jazz, let me hear what he has to say, then he will be gone," she says, lowering her gun and placing it in a holster she has at her back.

"You sure Mari, because I can take him," Jasmine says. I laugh to myself at this little feisty woman. She grabs her young and walks out of the room. Finally we're alone.

"You have five minutes, Showken," she says. I start to come close and she takes two steps back.

"First, I'm sorry for hurting you, I didn't mean to. Well, I wanted you to want me. You said you wouldn't see me any more. I thought if you saw me with someone else you would admit your true feelings." I take a deep breath, and continue. "I don't want anyone else but you, if you could have seen me the other night, let's just say my beast didn't like rejection. I really don't want you to hate me, I want you to give me a chance. I didn't sleep with that woman, I want you, Marilyn, I have never loved any woman, ever." Taking another breath, I look to see if she's truly listening, and she is. I chance a step towards her and she doesn't move. This is good. "I'm willing to do whatever it takes to gain your trust, and I won't stop until I get it back," I say, staring. I can't believe I used the word love. I'm not sure about that, but I'm sure about wanting her right now. She says nothing for a while. I can see wheels are turning in her head.

"I don't want you, I don't ever want to see you again. I was going to reconsider not seeing you, but you, you set out to make me jealous, to hurt me. I should have never trusted you anyway. So, do yourself a favor and leave me alone. Don't feel guilty about what happened. We had great sex and that was it. Now, if you respect me you will leave, now," she says, calmly. Fuck. I do respect her, but leaving her alone is not an option. I run my hands through my hair, pulling it tight. She is staring at me expressionlessly, yet I hear her heart rate increase, I see her eyes widening and I smell her arousal. She says she wants me to leave her alone, but that's not the truth. I'll give her some time.

"Marilyn, I'll go, for now, but make no mistake, I will not give up." I stop talking to inhale deeply. "You and I are not over, beautiful," I say, turning towards the door to leave. I will be with her very soon. Marilyn is quiet as I move towards the door. I turn and blow her a kiss.

MARILYN

Why is he doing this? I fall right down on my knees, burying my face in my hands to cry. I hear Jasmine come out the room. My God-daughter, Rachel, follows. I see her playing with Bruiser, and feel a small smile come. I love to see Rachel. Jasmine comes and sits with me on the floor. I sit for a few minutes and need to leave. I have to think. Showken says he won't leave me alone. Why? He doesn't even know me, and I don't know him.

"Jasmine," I say, rising from the floor. "Can Bruiser stay for a little while? I need to think. I promise I'm going home tonight. I just want to take a drive right now. I'll be back,"

"You okay, Mari? I was listening, and he sounds serious about not leaving you alone," Jasmine says.

"I know, that's the problem, he is serious." I look at Jasmine through my tears. "Jazz, seeing him today, I, I really don't know if I want to stop seeing him. That is why I need to think he could be a very good manipulator, right?" I ask.

"Right, unless he is the real thing, Mari. Keep your phone on and go take a quiet drive, and go with your first mind and I'll back you up no matter what," she says. Rachel comes over to me with her arms stretching up.

"I want up," she says. I pick her up, swinging her around, and she screams with laughter. I love her so much, and she loves me. I sit her down on the sofa and give her a kiss.

I pat and hug Bruiser, promising him I will be back to get him. I walk out the door and jump in my car and hit the road. No destination planed, just a drive.

I turn up the music and just drive. I can't get Showken out of my mind. His touch and kiss are amazing. I've never been so happy to have sex with anyone. Showken made me forget the horrible life I've had.

His words of "not leaving me alone" were soothing, Showken makes me feel pretty and desirable. Yet, he still hurt me, trying to make me jealous to get what he wanted was not right. Using me to fill their needs is what everyone does to me, except Jazz and Bruiser. I wish I had never met Showken.

Yes, he gave me mind-blowing sex and made me smile. I even felt happy, for a minute. My happiness vanished like smoke and now I'm hurting for this man, considering giving him another chance. It's my need for abuse, my mother always told me, "abuse will always follow you, Marilyn". She is a trying woman, who should never have gotten pregnant.

I turn down the music, seeing my phone ring. Shit, it's Showken. I'm not talking to him. I let the voicemail pick up. I breathe a sigh of relief. Then a text shows up on my screen:

Answer your phone beautiful, please.

Shit, why is he doing this? Showken makes it very difficult to say no to him with his stubbornness. I'm not texting back, that is wrong, and I took the pledge not to text and drive. The phone rings again. I answer, pushing the speaker button.

"I thought I told you to leave me alone!" I snap.

"I thought I told you, you and I are not over. Now sweetheart, can you pull over at that donut shop up ahead?" Showken asks.

"What? I'm not pulling . . . wait, did you say pull over? Are you following me? Shit, Showken, you are a stalker," I say, looking in my mirror when I see his Hummer.

"Marilyn, please. I can't stop thinking about you, I just want to talk, please," he begs. I can't believe him.

"Fine, I'm pulling over," I say, cutting off the person next to me and pulling over. I hear horns honking, I turn and see his Hummer cutting off people, too. I smile. He pulls his huge Hummer into the parking lot right next to me. He jumps out, and is at my passenger door knocking on the window. I roll it down a little.

"What?" I snap. He just stares at me. I don't want him in my car, that is way too close in this small space. "Showken, you're not getting in. Anything you have to say, you can say it standing right there." He's so quiet. His eyes are piercing me, and I hit the unlock button to get him to stop staring at me like that.

"Thank you, Marilyn, where are you going?" he asks, turning his body towards me. He is having difficulty, too. My car is way too small for him. I hold in a laugh, and focus on getting him out of my car.

"Showken, you can't follow me, this is not going to work. I can't trust you and-" I'm cut off, feeling soft lips on mine. I should be pulling away from him, yet my hands are instantly fisted in his hair and I pull hard. I'm angry that I want this kiss, and that he is taking a kiss.

This man is driving me crazy. He is sucking, biting, and licking my lips. I feel his hand move up my shirt, squeezing my breasts hard. I moan into his mouth, "Ahhh". His touch feels so good. He finally pulls away, leaving me panting.

"Come to my place with me right now, please," Showken says. His eyes flicker from his normal green to a different green, it's amazing.

"Showken, I have Bruiser. I need to go home, and we are not going to do this," I say, waving my hand between us.

"Bring him. There is plenty of room for him to walk around, and I will make you some food."

He leans in, showering me with multiple pecks on my mouth. I can't resist this man. "I need to make it up to you. Besides, I'm lots of fun and I'll even let you pick a movie," he says, smiling. I'm a sucker for his smile.

"Okay," I say. His smile widens and it's contagious, I'm smiling, too. "I have to go pick up Bruiser from Jasmine's place. Give me your address and I will come over in about an hour," I say, gathering my thoughts. I might just stand him up.

"No, I'll follow you, precious. You might not come over and I'm not taking any chances with you, since you ran last time," he says, arching a brow at me. Narrowing my eyes I glare at him, he is too good at reading me.

"Okay, I'll call Jasmine and tell her to have Bruiser's toys ready. I'll grab him and follow you," I say.

"I like that better. I will have to watch you, lady. If you're trying to get rid of me, good luck," he says, climbing out of the car and running back to jump in his Hummer. I pull out, heading for Jazz' place. I call on the way and tell her I'm going to talk with Showken tonight, and I'm coming to get Bruiser. All she says is "Make sure you apologize right and eat up all night," she is so nasty and outspoken.

I love her. She's proven to be a friend. One day I will tell her my entire life story instead of bits and pieces. I pick up Bruiser and follow Showken to a beautiful dream home. I can't believe he came to my place that night.

I'm not going to fit in. I'm not rich and don't know what spoon or fork goes with what. I'm poor or average, and, looking at this house, Showken is out of my league.

***

The inside of the house says rich. After Showken pats Bruiser and whispers in his ear, Bruiser takes off on a run. Shit, I can't pay for anything he breaks. Showken doesn't say anything to me, leading me to an enormous straight-out-of-the-magazine kitchen. I should not touch anything where my hands will leave smudges.

"Sexy, what are you thinking about?" Showken asks, coming to stand right in front of me. Damn, he smells amazing.

"It's Marilyn, and I'm thinking that I should not be here, but if we must, Bruiser will be hungry soon, and we need to be outside, so he can relieve himself." I say, looking around.

"I will make sure one of my brothers takes care of that, love. Why don't you belong here?" he frowns.

"Really? Showken, I'm not the woman you need. I mean, you are in a different world than me. I live normal, I budget my money, I sometimes eat hot dogs for dinner. This house says to me you have no idea about normal or eating hot dogs," I say. He cups my face and holds it gently in his hands.

"Marilyn, all of this means nothing to me. I'm not that kind of guy, I like normal and hot dogs, too, sometimes. But I want to get to know you better. I'm really an easy going guy, and what would you like to eat?" he asks, leaning down and capturing my mouth. He licks my lips until I open my mouth, and he takes full advantage. Our tongues are dancing. It feels so good. Finding my strength, I pull away. We stare at each other for a few seconds.

"I'm not having sex with you, Showken, you hurt me," I say, feeling my breathing is a little faster from that kiss.

"We don't have to have sex, beautiful, but can we cuddle when we watch a movie and eat? I like cuddling," he says, twisting his perfect mouth. I glare at him. "What would you like to eat?"

"Whatever you would like is fine with me. Did your brother take care of Bruiser, he needs food and water," I say.

"Really? I could make some chocolate cupcakes, and yes, Bruiser has been fed and he's playing now." I narrow my eyes and he lets out a loud laugh. "I could also make some sub sandwiches," he says, giving me a full-blown smile. I swallow hard; Showken is trying to test me with those smiles.

"Sub sandwiches will be great," I say. I take a seat at the counter, watching Showken pull out lunch-meat, veggies, cheese, and Sub buns. He is like a chef making these sandwiches. I'm watching him when two guys come into the kitchen. He stops and they all stare at each other. You would think an unspoken conversation was going on, with the looks they are giving each other. Finally the one with brown hair speaks. He is good-looking, too, but the other one, although he looks angry, is freaking beautiful.

"Hello Marilyn, it's nice to see you again. I'm Hawken, but you can call me Hawk," he says, stretching out his hand.

"Hello, Hawk," I say. I hear a rumble, or a loud plane passing, but we are not near the airport. The other brother speaks.

"I'm Domlen, Marilyn," he says, and I am captivated by his presence. His eyes are a weird, but beautiful, reddish color. I've never seen eyes like this.

"Domlen, Hawken, please don't scare my lady. Beautiful, pay no attention to them. They know how I can become a crazy animal," Showken says, smiling, but his eyes say he is pissed. Another one walks in and he's fine, too. "Marilyn, these are my brothers, Hawken, Domlen, and Layern."

"Nice to meet you all, brothers, wow," I say. Layern comes and sits right next to me.

"Showken, subs, great, I love subs. Thank you, brother," Layern says. Shit, brother, what kind of talk is that?

"I'm making Marilyn and me subs. I think you guys can find something else to eat," he says, clenching his teeth. He sounds upset, not five minutes have passed and his mood is changed.

"There is a dog sleeping in front of your bedroom door," Hawken says. He looks at me then.

"Yes, it's my dog and his name is Bruiser, and don't bother him, or he will bite," I warn them, although Bruiser is slacking, like the other night with Showken.

"Bite? Marilyn, we bite back," Layern says, reaching over the counter and grabbing an apple out of the fruit bowl on the island.

"Enough. Baby, you ready to watch a movie?" Showken asks, looking into my eyes. Shit, he's a fine man.

"Umm, yes. I think I know what I want to watch, too," I say, giving nothing away about the movie. He raises a brow at me and gives me that smile, it's truly like sunshine. He makes a tray with about five subs, two bags of chips, and a bottle of wine. It seems like he will drop something. I try to help, but he insists that I just follow him. We walk into a theater room. It's beautiful, with four rows of leather love seats and smooth, red carpet. In front of each sofa is a perfect sized table for food, snacks, and a drink. There are even curtains on the side of the wall. I'm so out of my league. I swallow hard. I shouldn't be here, Showken hurt me, and I said I was not going to see him, yet here I stand.

"Pick a row, Marilyn, and tell me the movie we are watching, so I can get it started," Showken says. I head to the second row and get comfy on the seats. They feel amazing. I decide to take my shoes off, and curled up on the love seat. He places the food in front of me, producing two wine glasses. How the hell did he carry all this without anything falling? "Beautiful, name of movie, please."

"Oh, do you have The Notebook?" I ask.

"Yes, I do." Showken smiles, walking towards the back dimming the lights, and the movie is starting. He comes and sits down, lifting my feet onto his lap. He picks up one of the sub sandwiches and pushes it into my mouth.

"Take a bite, lady," he insists. I take a bite, and even in the dark I see his eyes on me. "You are so beautiful," he says, pulling me closer to watch the movie. He pours us glasses of wine, and we cuddle, not saying a word, watching the movie. Showken is such a gentleman, he doesn't try anything, in fact, I think he is watching the movie, too. The end of the movie finally comes, and I'm crying. I love this movie, and cry every time I watch it. Showken grabs a remote I didn't notice, and turns the lights up some. It's still pretty dim, though. I look at the table and all the subs are gone. I feel his eyes on me, noticing I'm lying on his chest.

"I'm sorry," Showken says. "I'm so sorry for hurting you. I didn't mean to, you have to believe that. I like you very much, I want you real bad, and would like it if you would stay." Stay where? Here in this mansion, I don't think so. I need to go home. If I stay, sex will be involved, and I'm not strong enough to resist Showken.

"Showken, I accept your apology, but I'm not ready to get involved with you. I think I should go home," I say, pulling away. I feel his arms tighten around me, and I inhale his beautiful smell. He takes a deep breath, pulling me onto his lap so that now I'm straddling him. He gently, slowly lowers his head to my chest, taking in deep breaths. His hands start massaging up and down my back, giving me shivers.

"Please, I need you," he says, as he slowly starts to kiss my neck. I close my eyes, enjoying his touch. Everything on my body is heated. I think my hands are even hot. His hands start to move up my shirt, finding their way to my aching breasts. My back automatically arches lifting my breasts towards his hands. He tortures me, barely touching my hardened nipples. Before I can think, he is kissing me hard and fast. I can't stop. He pulls away and looks at me, his eyes bright; the green is intense, and sexy as hell.

"Stay the night with me, Marilyn, please," he pleads. Tilting his head, he starts to lick and suck my neck. Everything inside me is melting like ice cream.

"Showken, oh Showken, I thought we agreed no sex."

"I never agreed to that. I said we don't have to have sex, doesn't mean I don't want to. Beautiful, I want you so bad right here, right now, say yes." He places his hands on my thighs, his thumb rubbing my inner thigh. I shake my head, trying to gain some strength, but my walls are crumbling. A moan betrays me. "Mmmm".

"Yes, love, just feel, don't think," Showken says, his fingers gliding up and down my, now very hot, sex.

"Showken," I whisper.

"Yes."

"I, I, yes." The words leave my mouth before I can think. Showken moves quickly in front of me, getting onto his knees. He keeps his eyes on me. They are truly beautiful. I can't believe a man like this wants me. He pulls off my pants, slowly and gently. He's in no rush. I gasp, feeling heat between us. He climbs up my body and pushes the back of the sofa, and it starts lowering down. Damn I've never seen this before. I'm lying down now. Showken lifts up, pulling his shirt over his head. Oh that chest is amazing.

"I want you so bad, Marilyn, I feel like I'm going to explode," he says, pushing my legs apart. My panting is getting louder now. I can't believe I react this way with this man. He slides my panties off, kissing me until he reaches my feet. This man is too good to be true. He begins to suck and bite each one of my toes, I cry out in pleasure, "Ahhhhh". Showken doesn't stop. He starts sucking my hip where it meets my pelvic bone. Licking and kissing, making everything south go extremely wet. I can believe how hot I am. "Beautiful, I want you to release, so I can have some dessert," he says, pulling my folds apart, he starts licking me with long fast strokes from my opening to my clitoris. This is crazy, I've had many men in my life, but Showken makes me feel like I've never made love before. His tongue now slides into my sex and I scream loudly. Bruiser's barking comes next, and then I remember his brothers and place my hand over my mouth. I should have better control. Showken whispers that Bruiser will be alright. He pulls my hand down by my side, holding my hands on my thighs as he keeps my legs apart with his shoulders. Holding me still, he starts again, sliding his tongue in . . . out . . . in . . . out of my sex. My head is moving from side to side. I yell out "SHOOOWKEN!" I release, just as he asked. He sucks hard, making my orgasm last longer. My body is shaking and I've never felt this good in my life, ever.

"Precious, you taste so good," he says, planting kisses on my clitoris. Oh, God, he's going to start again.

"Showken, please," I manage to gasp, in between panting. I can't even breathe. He's driving me crazy.

"Yes, I want more, and yes you will release again," he says, moving his tongue very fast over my clitoris before taking it in his mouth. I feel my body getting hotter. I can't believe I'm going to have another, "Oh, Oh, Ohhhhhhh," I yell out again. He comes up my body, stopping to take his time with my breasts. My nipples feel like fire every time he sucks, not a bad heat but a heat that's so good. I want to get up and make a run for the door. This feels way too good.

SHOWKEN

I can't control myself around Marilyn. She brings feelings out of me that should not be there. Her body is gorgeous, and extremely tempting. Watching the movie with her cuddling against me is making me want her more; the movie won't end fast enough. She tastes amazing. Her sweet, intoxicating natural juice is my addiction. I feel Hawken and Layern nudging at my head to watch. I usually let my brothers see, and have even let them feel sometimes, but Marilyn is different. I can't let them see her. She has an amazing body, I'm not like Draken, it's just that I know she would be offended, and that offends me. I feel like she could be my Wella. I hate even thinking like that. I don't want a Wella, not now, but Marilyn is so addictive I can't get enough. I slide my pants down fast, wrapping her legs around me I thrust inside her body. I've never wanted to yell out, but this feels so good, her body is perfect for me. I can't share her with another man, even if she's not my Wella. Her breasts are perfect and fit my hand. Those hips and ass make me want never to stop holding them. Giving her pleasure is my pleasure. I love her eyes rolling around, searching for an explanation of why. I need her from behind.

"Beautiful, turn around for me," I ask, rising so that she can. "You have the most perfect ass I've ever seen. You are going to have to let me have this part of you, someday," I say, planting soft kisses on each cheek. I grab her ass hard, and I growl. My beast likes it, too. I hear her moan, "Ahhhh, Showken," she says, with a trembling voice. I love her moans of pleasure. I place two fingers inside her sex, sliding them in and out, I bend and open that ass, circling her body with my tongue. She screams out with such satisfaction. "Ohhhhhh, YESSS," she yells. She starts to pump against my hands as I slide my fingers in and out. I smile hearing that, she likes this. When I get that ass, I might scream, too. I slide my fingers out, placing them in my mouth, sucking her juice, which is now my addiction. I thrust inside again, going slow, fast, and hard. I can't be gentle, I want her to have it all. She is smacking that ass up against me, and my thoughts are all over the place.

"Yes, Showken, feels so . . . ohh . . . good!"

I can't speak. If I let anything out right now, I'm going to let out a very scary growl. I bite down, holding my breath as long as possible. I bend, licking her back as she meets me with each thrust. She feels so good. I allow my heat to come to my tongue; now, as I lick her back, the heat will increase her need. It will give her more intense orgasms, and leave a green line down her back. I hope she doesn't mind. I smile, knowing I want my marks on her body, everywhere. I rise up, lifting her body with me. She rests her head on my chest as her body is pressed against me. I reach around with one hand pulling her nipple, continuing my pumping into her sweet sex. I love her sounds. "Scream for me, baby." That must turn her on, because her cry touches my inner core. "Whyyyyy meeeee!" she yells.

I slow down my pace, giving her a chance to recover. I start biting her right ear, and lightly sticking my tongue inside. Calming my beast is a must right now.

"Marilyn, it's you, because you're special," I say, in between kissing her neck. "You. Are. So. Special. But. Most. Of. All. Beautiful," I say with each kiss. I rub my hands down the front of her body.

"I need a break, Showken, please," she says, panting. I hear and feel her heart beat. The sweat is dripping off her body. I lay her down gently, sliding out. I lie facing her on the sofa. With my dragon eyes, I can see everything on her body. She finally catches her breath, running her hands through her hair and closing her eyes. I see tears starting to stream down her face, sliding into her mouth. Why is she crying?

"Love-"

Marilyn places her finger to my mouth to quiet me.

"Showken, this is moving so fast. I don't want this. I'm not ready for this, you are easy to fall for, and I'm not ready," she says. I narrow my eyes, feeling anger come over me. I will not let her go. She will not be with another man, she's mine.

"Marilyn . . . you, okay, I'm not sure if you understand. We can take this slowly, but you getting off this between us will not happen." I lean in, taking her bottom lip, pulling gently on it. "I don't take rejection well, in fact I won't accept it," I say, smelling her. I love her smell, her smell mixed with mine is right. I don't give her a chance to talk, I stand, pulling her into my arms. I carry her to my room. I'm kissing her the entire time. When she notices the change in the room, chuckling is all I can do. She looks adorable, being surprised. I walk over to my bed. We fall on the bed together, and I see her smile. I could get used to seeing that smile all the time. I decide to let her sleep a little. She falls asleep quickly once we are in the bed together. I slide out of the bed, slipping on a pair of sweats, heading for food. I open the door and Bruiser is sleeping, too. I pat him and keep moving. I get to the kitchen and see Layern eating a family-sized box of cereal.

"You love her," he says, instantly. I hear him crunching, I see it's my cereal.

"Shit, Layern. You know the rule, you eat your own food, no eating others' unless you ask," I say, going to the fridge, grabbing fruit, cheese and chicken from the last night Hawken cooked. If

Layern is eating my food, well, I'm eating others' food. It's called sharing the love.

"Well, you didn't let us see, so I got hungry. I had no more cereal, but you did. Now, you love her, please don't lie," Layern says.

"I don't know what it is, Layern, I've never loved a woman before," I say, smiling, remembering how being inside Marilyn is like paradise.

"You okay, I mean, you know, with your beast?" he asks, raising his eyes to meet mine. I stop eating, grinning. I feel great, as long as Marilyn doesn't try to run.

"I feel good, so does my beast. Mother would not have sent me back if she thought different," I say, raising a brow.

"Okay, what are you going to do? She's not your usual one night stand, and I get the feeling you don't want her to go anywhere. She will soon find out how jealous the green monster can be," Layern says, shoveling down cereal like a maniac.

"Layern, I said that I'm fine, but if you keep talking about my beast you will see my green monster," I smile.

"Whatever, I've seen it before, but how will Marilyn react, knowing you have a crazy temper?" he asks, getting up and putting his bowl in the sink.

"I have it under control, brother, but you doubting me is upsetting my beast," I say, glaring. He glares back, then smiles. Layern doesn't smile. I guess he is truly back. I'm happy for him, but he is pushing me, is he trying to get me to lose control? I will not.

"Don't get angry, Showken. Yes, I'm back. I feel good, but I still love her. I can say I love her. Can you say you love Marilyn?" he says, walking out of the kitchen. I think for a second and the only answer is, no. I want her, she's addictive, but love is not for me. I just want her around longer.

"Brother, this has nothing to do with love; I like Marilyn's company right now. My mind could change tomorrow, you know me," I say, trying to convince myself more than Layern.

"Yes, I do know you, now you should be honest with yourself, brother," he says, continuing down the hall. I sit and eat more food. Mother wants to meet Marilyn, but I'm not sure if that's a good idea. Marilyn's mouth will get her into trouble with my mother. Why does she want to see her anyway? I'm not ready for a Wella. I finish eating, and quickly make Marilyn some food. I head back into the room and she's still sound asleep. I would love to be in her dream. I usually don't like entering women's dreams, especially after they have been with me sexually. They have a wedding and everything planned out. I'm not sure if Marilyn is that type, only one way to find out. Besides, my dragon wants to meet her officially, and she might consider this a nightmare. I go and climb into bed with her, wrapping my arms around her waist. Closing my eyes, I drift into her dream.

I can't believe what I'm seeing, Marilyn is in a room sitting on a couch, with a knife in her hand and blood on her clothes. She looks cold, her eyes are somewhat dilated, and she's calm. I glance over and see a man on the floor with several stab wounds. Shit, she's a killer! I see her walk out of the room and take a shower. I'm really going to have to investigate this further. This is not in her file at all. Her dream shifts and she's on a cliff, sitting on the edge, looking at something in the distance. I make my presence known, and walk up behind her, taking a seat on the cliff with her. She doesn't look my way.

"Why are you in my dreams? I'm not as good as you think?" she asks calmly. I frown, wondering why she is so calm, and her tone so cold.

"I'm here because you wanted me, it's your dream, tell me why I'm here, precious," I say. I need to get some truths out of her, this dream may be my only chance.

"Showken, I'm not sure how you are in my dream. I try to keep this to myself, but it's a dream." She takes a huge breath, letting it out very slowly. "I come onto this cliff to think. I even sometimes think about jumping, my life is lonely. I have no one, really." She stops looking over the horizon, narrowing her eyes, and turns to me, just looking.

"I'm no good for you, I'm not good for anyone, and you should run," she says, lowering her head. I guess she needs to see me fully. I call for my dragon and I see him flying in. I see her lean forward, and I can't help but smile. She thinks she's a bad person, well I'm not even all human. She stands as my dragon approaches. Marilyn takes two steps back, as she can now fully see what is coming fast towards her.

"Beautiful, why are you stepping back?" I ask, knowing there is fear coming over her. My beast can be very scary, but I control it, she'll be fine.

"Umm, Showken, I think you should step back, too. I know this is a dream, but this is turning into a nightmare, come, lets go," she says, reaching for me. I pull her back down, wrapping my arms around her.

"It's okay, he just wants to meet you," I say, looking for her reaction.

"What do you mean? Showken, this big bird with wings looks like some myth, you're scaring me," she says, looking at the beast, which is now hovering right in front of the cliff. I feel her body stiffen. I feel my body get aroused, my beast loves her. "Wait, you know this bird?"

"Would you please stop calling it a bird," I say, widening my eyes. My beast shoots out fire that sends her stumbling, trying to get away.

"Fuck, Showken, this is crazy. What is going on?"

"Sweetie, it's fine, he's fine. What do you think is going on?" I ask. Holding her from behind now, I secure her arms, and we are facing my beast.

"I think you know this, this, shit, what is it? This must be my punishment, dying in my dream, being eaten by a very large flying, fire-spitting . . . holy shit, it's a dragon! Fuck that, wake up, Oh God, I'm sorry, wake up, Marilyn." She starts to panic. I nod, sending my dragon away to fly in the sky until I can get her under control. I still hear her pleading with God to wake her up from her dream.

"Relax, you're making him nervous, which makes me nervous. That's me and I'm him, we are one," I say, resting my chin on her shoulder. She looks at my beautiful green monster, frowning, then I see understanding sinking in, and hold her tight. She starts to pull away. I let go and because she is so rattled, she slips off the cliff. "AHHHHHHHHHHHHHHH!" she yells, as she falls. My beast comes and flies under her to catch her. She is holding on tight; I can feel the grip on my shoulders.

"I THOUGHT YOU WERE SCARED!" I yell, as I command my beast to take her for a ride. She holds on to the necklace around my beast. She yells back.

"I AM SCARED!" she yells, with a small smile. She's enjoying herself. I smile to myself, WOW! She's an amazing lady. I take a step back and run to the edge, taking a jump off, my beast knowing to be right there. I climb on behind her, and we fly.

"How are you feeling?" I ask.

"Well, it's a dream, but I feel free, and the view is really nice," she says, as the wind is blowing that dark hair in her face. I brush it out of the way, and grabbing her face with both hands, I lean in, kissing her hard.

"I love to fly, and it's very liberating," I say, pulling away to see her face. She looks confused.

"Is this real?"

"Do you want it to be?"

She looks out over the clouds, enjoying the beauty, I assume.

"Yes, I do." We stare at each other for a long time. I pull her close and we ride in silence. This is wrong. She can't love me, I can love her . . . I do love her, but loving me is dangerous. My beast can get crazy sometimes. I can't have her injured because of me. Inhaling her beautiful scent changes my focus. My hands slide up her shirt, and I find her hard nipples. Her gasps become my incentive to do more, as I'm kissing her neck. I love pleasing her. The sounds she makes are very arousing. I want her right now, but I won't do that. She leans back on my chest, opening her body to me. She must not care about my beast, or she's forgotten. Sliding my hand to her hot, wet sex, I slip in a finger, sliding it in, out, in, out. After I add two more fingers, she finds her release. "YESSSSSS!" she yells. It's almost enough to make me climax. I can't believe what I'm doing. My mother would like to meet her. I need to figure that out. Marilyn is no pushover, and my mother- let's just say after someone's spoken with her I've seen their ashes left.

"Marilyn, are you ready to wake up?" I ask, smiling into her neck. I know she doesn't want to wake, but she must. I can't keep her in dreamland, though the thought is enticing, I won't do that.

"Well, no, but I know it's a dream, and nothing good ever lasts for me. Since this is a dream, I want you to know that this won't last between us. We should end it before it goes further," she says, calmly.

"I'm not ready for it to end, and I'm selfish by nature," I say, feeling a growl come, running my hand through my hair. I can't hold back, and I growl loudly, my beast joins in and fire comes from his mouth. I will end it when I'm ready, not her. Layern is right; I do love her, and letting go right now is not an option. I need more of her, besides, a human female will never be able to handle me or my beast.

"Showken, let's just enjoy this ride on this big bird dragon thingy," she says, sighing. I look over the horizon. I feel the pull to come back, and I let Marilyn rest her head on my shoulder as she drifts off in her dream. This is my chance to bring her back from this dream. I kiss the top on her head, and closing my eyes, I return to my room. I need to think of my next move.

MARILYN

My eyes pop right open. I've never had a dream like that. I look over and see Showken sleeping next to me. He looks amazing. His dimples are even noticeable in his sleep. I see there's a tray of food on the table next to me. There is cheese, crackers, fruit, chocolates, veggies and breads with jams. WOW! Never had a guy be so concerned with my food. I'm taking a bite of chocolate and my mind can't get past that dream. Showken shows up on my cliff, and so does a green scary dragon. I can't forget how big it was. I'm glad it was a dream, although Showken made me orgasm in my dream. I look under the covers and notice the wetness between my legs. Feeling eyes on me, I look over my shoulder and see those green eyes and dimples. Oh!

"What time is it?" I ask, trying to disguise my need for him.

"It's late at night, just after midnight, I'm glad you're eating. Can I have some?" he says, pulling me close to him. "Mmmmm, I love your ass on me."

"Ahh, yes, you can have some food," I say. He chuckles into my hair. He reaches over my shoulder and grabs some fruit, stuffing his mouth. This guy is unreal. My mind drifts back to my dream. "I had a strange dream," I say. He looks me in the eyes and smiles.

"What did you dream, love?" he asks, relaxing his body.

"You were in my dream, with a big bird dragon thingy, and we flew on its back," I say. I feel really stupid now that I say it out loud, until he speaks.

"It's either a dragon or a bird, but not both. Did you enjoy the dream?" he says, looking me in the eyes, not blinking. His eyes almost remind me of, shit . . . fuck. It can't be.

"Showken, I feel like you already know about it, your eyes . . . I should go home," I say, getting ready to lift the cover, but he's at my ear. "Be still, Marilyn, you are not leaving this time. Besides, we are having fun, and I want to give you at least four more orgasms tonight," he says. Lowering his head, he starts licking my back. It feels so good.

"Umm, okay, I should at least call Jasmine. I promised I would call her." He looks at me, narrowing his eyes.

"Okay, I'll get your cell phone; as you already know, walking is out right now." He climbs out of bed, fully erect. My mouth goes dry, but I need to let Jasmine know I'm okay. I did tell her I would when I picked up Bruiser. Oh damn, where is Bruiser?

"Umm, Bruiser, where is he?" I ask.

"Bruiser is sleeping, but he won't be able to hear us, I'm a man of many talents, so don't hold your screams in," he says, handing me my cell phone. He slips out of his sweat pants. I want him in my mouth. I lick my lips, feeling a growing need.

"Thanks for the information," I whisper, turning my head away from him. I hit one on my phone, dialing Jasmine's number.

"Hello Mari, how's everything going?" she asks. I feel Showken positioning himself between my legs. My eyes go big, no he can't do this while I'm on the phone. I shake my head very fast.

"Umm, it's going good. Umm, OH!" I say, feeling something cold being placed in between my folds. What is that?

"Well, did you kiss and make up?" she says, all excited. Jazz, if you only knew, is my thought.

"Umm, mmm, yes we did. It's amazing!" I shout out. Showken looks up and he has chocolate on his mouth, damn, I've got chocolate in my doodah.

"Mari, are you screwing?" Jasmine asks. I can't talk. Showken is laughing at me and devouring my sex.

"Umm, Yesssss!" I yell, in ecstasy.

"Well, hot fudge on a Popsicle stick, have fun, bye," she says, laughing, and hangs up the phone. Showken really goes to work, I'm sure he heard Jazz' big mouth. He starts sucking my sex so hard I hear his mouth make a popping sound when he releases. I'm pulling his hair now, I can't be still. My hips are jumping. He holds my hips in place, so he can start sucking my clitoris. I feel my release coming, he does, too. He's at my entrance with his tongue moving in and out. My release comes, and I can't stop the scream that escapes my mouth. Showken is on top of me fast, kissing me. I open my mouth to feel his tongue; our tongues dance together. I taste myself and chocolate. I feel his sex on my entrance, while staring into my eyes, he pushes inside me. I gasp at the feeling.

"Don't leave me, please," he says. His eyes are pleading.

"Okay," is my only response. I know I can't stay, but I will enjoy him for a little while.

We make love for the rest of the night. I cry some of the time, but no words are exchanged. I can't believe it. I think I love him, and soon I will have to walk away.

***

The morning is here. I'm naked in bed with Showken, feeling good, but tired. I need sleep. I rub his head, loving his beautiful hair. What man's hair is so beautiful? I look at my cell phone on the table and it's just after 6:00 a.m. I need to get up, but I don't want to be on the floor again.

"Good morning, sexy. I assume you need the bathroom," he says, chuckling.

"Yes, you are assuming right," I say, smiling. He climbs out of the bed, naked. I had almost forgotten I needed the bathroom, until the cover comes off and the need to pee comes over me. He lifts me like I'm a doll and walks me into the bathroom, seating me on the toilet. His bathroom is huge. I walk over to his gigantic tub. He starts the water and pours a green liquid into the tub. He walks back over to me smiling. This man is not real. I'm going to wake up soon, I just know it. He is too good to be true.

"You ready for your bath, beautiful?" My mouth is open. I grab the tissue and wipe myself. The toilet flushes automatically. Showken leans down and picks me up. He carries me to the tub, and he steps in and sits, with me in his arms. I try to move, but he doesn't let me.

"Relax, I've got you. I'm sure you need to relax," he says, turning my body slowly so that my back is up against his hard chest. I wince some, as I am sore.

"Showken, you have to stop spoiling me, I may not want to go home," I say, joking. I think.

"Then don't. You can stay, Marilyn, in fact I would like that," he says, grabbing what looks like shampoo. He squeezes a nice amount into his hand and starts to massage my head. He pushes me down his body until my hair is in the water, and pulls me back. The massage on my head is fantastic.

"I can't stay here, I'm going home this morning. I need to go home," I say. His hands still on my head, then he continues the massage.

"If you go home, can I come over later?" he says. Sliding me forward, he stands, taking me with him. He turns the shower on and turns me towards him. I lean back into the warm water. I rinse my hair. I grab some body wash. I can't look him in the eyes. I know that when I leave here, seeing him again will not be in my, or his, best interest. He is in the public eye, being with me will tarnish that, being as how I'm an ex-prostitute and murderer. We shower together like a couple. I've regained my strength, and after drying my body I put my clothes back on, excluding my panties. They are stained with my juices.

"Precious, your hair is still damp, let me dry it? I only ask that you close your eyes," he says, raising a brow. I nod okay, and sit in the green velvet chair by the bathroom door. I close my eyes, feeling his hands in my hair. I hear the dryer turn on. I feel the hot air on my head; this is a great dryer. In a minute my hair is dry. I open my eyes and the dryer is in his hand.

"Thank you," I say, feeling like he wants to laugh.

"You're welcome, beautiful, before you leave, breakfast, please? I'm going to go to work after you leave," he says, reaching for my hand.

"Breakfast, then I go home," I say, smiling.

"Everyone is waiting," he says, walking me out of the room. What does he mean everyone is waiting, fuck! I don't want to eat with everyone. We walk into this huge, all white room. I giggle to myself. Why the damn white room. I laugh more, shaking my head. I open my eyes and all his brothers are standing, looking at me. Oh shit.

"Sorry," I say, not even knowing why I'm apologizing.

"You're fine, let's eat," Showken says. We get to the table and the head seat is empty. I thought Showken was going to sit there, but he doesn't, he takes the seat next to it, and I'm seated next to him.

"Who else is coming?" I whisper.

"That's our oldest brother's seat, no one sits there except him," Showken says. I don't ask anything else. He starts to fix my plate, loading it with eggs, sausage, fruit, toast, and strawberry jam.

"So, Marilyn . . . " Layern starts.

"Shut up, Layern. She's my company, and don't ask her anything," Showken says, in a frightening tone. Another brother speaks up.

"Well, our mother called, she says you are on a time limit."

"OK, HAWKEN!" Showken yells. I stuff my mouth with eggs. I need to go, shit this is intense. I stand, grabbing a piece of toast. I'm getting the hell out of here.

"Where are you going?" Showken asks, grabbing my arm. He doesn't look up at me, he is glaring at his brother, and I'm pretty sure I hear growling

"I'm going home, I, I don't want any more to eat," I say, feeling a little shaky. His grip is strong.

"Please sit, my brothers are sorry for scaring you," he says, through his teeth.

"Umm, I'm not scared. Bruiser!" I yell. He shows up next to me. Showken won't let go.

"Please, please, breakfast, remember," he pleads. I sigh out loud. I see all eyes are on me.

"Marilyn, I don't like my brother begging, so will you do him the honor and give him some respect and sit down," Domlen says. I can't believe I remember his name, but more importantly, Domlen just spoke to me in a no nonsense tone. We stare at each other, and I find myself sitting back down.

"Thank you, beautiful. Thank you," Showken says, continuing to eat. The silence in the room is thick. There is some unspoken message among them. They all look at each other, and glance at me. I grab the orange juice, and wonder what could be so important about me staying for breakfast. I will just sit and eat some fruit.

Finally I make it home. Bruiser and I go snuggle on the sofa. I can't believe these last couple of days. Being with Showken is nice, but I don't belong. How am I going to get Showken to back off? He tracked me down and followed me. I look at Bruiser, hoping for an answer, but he just looks at me. He likes Showken. "Bruiser, it's going to be you and me again," I say, rubbing his head. My cell starts buzzing, and I know it's a text from the sound. I get up and check to see who it is. I used to know who would text me, but since Showken that has changed.

Are you home yet?

The text is from Jazz.

Yes but I'm not talking on the phone. Text whatever questions you have.

I just don't feel like talking, besides this way I can control Jazz a little. She wants details of me and Showken.

Fine, is your doodah sore? He looks like he can make a doodah sore. Lol.

I shake my head, knowing only Jazz would ask something like that. She's shameless.

Yes, I'm sore but I took a bath and yes he can make a doodah sore. Lol He's the BEST I've ever had.

I wait for the reply. It takes a minute then it comes through.

THE BEST!!!! I want some of that action. Hook me up with a brother I hope it runs in the family. I can't believe you got a hot shot billionaire chasing your ass. I mean not that you don't deserve it. I'm so freaking happy for you. Is his house the shit?

I laugh out loud reading Jazz' text. She's so crazy. She's not going to like what I text back.

Well, I've decided not to see him anymore, and before you go all crazy. I think it's for the best. I'm not the woman he needs. He's not for me. Soon he will get bored and I have to protect my heart but I will try and hook you up with Layern. The other two I don't think so one is an asshole and the other is a bigger asshole.

I wait for Jazz' text to come. When I get another text coming through, I see it's from Showken, shit. Jazz' text dings.

If you break up with him over some stupid shit like that then I'm going to choke you. Just have fun and if it

ends it ends. **Now which one is Layern?**

I type back fast.

Showken just texted me. I will consider your suggestion and Layern is the really good dancer. ttyl

I open Showken's text right away. I feel butterflies in my gut.

Hello beautiful, I can't stop thinking about last night or this morning. I want to see you again tonight, I can pick you and Bruiser up at 7:00 p.m. I got a long day at work. Please say yes, I have a surprise for you, sexy.

Shit, I'm trying to get away, and he can't stay away. Do I want to see him?

Showken I think I should stay at home. I need some space to think ok.

I walk over to my kitchen and open the fridge, just looking. I'm nervous about his response. I usually don't care about people, especially a man's response, but Showken is different. My cell dings.

I'm in a meeting right now or I would be coming over. I'm not letting you go beautiful, now put on something nice I have a surprise for you. You don't need space you only think you do. Don't try to run, I'll find you. 7:00 p.m. please be ready.

I guess the decision is made. My mind is spinning as I stare at the text in shock. I can't believe him. What is this surprise? It must be important because he's even told me what to wear. I smile a little, feeling special that someone wants to surprise me. I will see him one last time, I hope. I text back:

Fine, I'll be ready at 7pm but don't make this a habit. I do need space.

I head towards the room to pick out a dress and my cell dings again.

No space.

I shake my head as I enter my room. He said Bruiser and me. Where are we going? I'm not the dress type of girl. I own three dresses, one black, one orange, and one flowered. I'm not liking my choices. I need to call for Jazz. She has plenty of dresses.

After I speak with Jazz and she stops over with ten dresses to choose from, we both decide on this very light green, off the shoulder, knee length dress. She has brought her makeup and some shoes and a purse to match. We laugh and giggle about my night, and how he makes sure I can't walk after sex. Around about 5:00 p.m. Jazz and Rachel leave and I prepare for this surprise. I have given Bruiser a bath earlier, so he is clean. As my bath is running, I can't help but think of Showken. He's made my bath water twice, and carried me to it. I shake my head. What man carries a woman to the tub after sex? I've only known losers all my life, even my father. I've never met a man like Showken. Shaking off the feeling, I continue to get ready for this date. I'm done at 6:50 p.m. An anxious feeling is in my gut. What if I don't fit in? What if he changes his mind? My heart is beating fast, I should just not open the door. This is- there is a knock at my door. Walking to the door holding my breath, I open it.

"Oh, you look fabulous, and that color on you makes naughty thoughts come to mind," Showken says, placing his hands on my hips. He looks amazing with some black slacks on, white shirt, no tie, and his hair neatly pulled into a ponytail. He looks like a Greek god.

"Thank you, you look nice, too," I say, blushing at his intense stare at me. His eyes are moving all over my body. "So what's the surprise?" I ask.

"Oh, there is someone I would like you to meet, come, we don't want to be late," he says, pulling me through the door, and snapping his fingers for Bruiser to follow. What restaurant is going to allow my dog?

"Showken, who do you want me to meet?" I ask, as we head towards his Hummer. He opens the back door and Bruiser jumps in. He opens the door for me. I climb in, wondering when he is going to answer. He gets in and pulls out.

"My mother," he simply says. Why the hell is he taking me to meet his mother?

"I don't want to meet your mother, Showken, turn the car around!" I snap. This is getting too serious. His mother is going to hate me.

"Beautiful, I can't cancel. My mother will not allow that, besides, she knows about you, and everything will be fine, I promise." He narrows his eyes. It feels like he's nervous. Shit.

"Showken, I don't care if your mother gets upset, turn around and take me home!" I yell. I'm nervous now. Why does he feel the need for me to meet his mother?

"Precious, Marilyn, calm down. It's just dinner, that's all. You mean a lot to me. I want you to meet my mother; I want you to know that I'm not playing games with you. I want you in my life and you need to meet my mother, so beautiful, take a deep breath and relax. You will be fine." He gives me a huge smile, and my mind eases some. He's so calm now.

"Ok, I'll meet your mother, Showken, but I want you to know I'm not pleased with this surprise," I say.

"Aww baby, I promise to make it up to you," he says. He voice is deep and sexy. Shit, my panties are going to be wet before we get to dinner. I don't say anything else for the entire ride. We pull up to a very fancy restaurant, but it looks closed.

"We own the restaurant, tonight it's just you, me, Bruiser, and Mother," he says, pulling up. We get out of the car and walk through the door. It's not what I'm expecting. It looks like we are outside in a garden. There's no roof on the building, so it looks like the sky is actually inside. It's beautiful, extremely beautiful. We walk in and there are flowers, tables with fruit and desserts everywhere. This is some restaurant. I've never seen a place like this. It feels like we are somewhere else. There is a woman with beautiful hair, wearing a long, flowing gown. She turns slightly, and she's beautiful. Showken reaches for my hand and waves for Bruiser to run, and he does. I smile, knowing how much he loves to play. We finally reach her table. She doesn't look up, as she is peeling some fruit or something. I've never seen it before. She sighs, lifting her head.

"So, you are the one who has stolen my son's heart. You don't look that special."

SHOWKEN

FUCK! I didn't expect my mother to say something like that to Marilyn. I'm not sure if this is a test or not, but I know that Queen Nala will always speak her mind. Marilyn's mouth is open, and she looks furious. Mother gave me a time limit, and time is up. The smile on my mother's face looks pure. I stare at my mother with my eyes widening. I know my beast is angry, calming down is mandatory. I can only go so far with my mother, but this is not right. Marilyn is very special to me.

"Mother, I-" Marilyn is speaking before I can finish my thought. Her fists are balled up, and she is all the way in fight mode. WOW!

"I didn't want to come to meet you, in fact I told him to turn around, but he said it would be fine. Showken is such a loving person. I may not be special or even good enough for your son, but don't ever speak to me like that again you BITCH! I know I'm not special, but you saying it out loud just confirms to me that ending it with Showken is best." She turns to leave, stopping at the door. I can't speak, my mother had better fix this quick. The heat of my beast is bringing smoke around my hands, and out of my mouth. My mother's eyes connect with mine.

"Wait! I said that you don't look that special, not that you are not special. I see you have a temper, and if you walk out of that door you are not worthy of my son. I've never met a woman he's bedded and ever cared for, until now. You have my son in knots about you." My mother sighs, and stands. Marilyn hasn't turned around the entire time she has been speaking. "If I offend you, I'm sorry. I just never thought Showken would be in love right now. Please, come, sit and eat with me." Queen Nala says sorry. I can't believe my ears. This is a first. I've never heard her say that ever, not even if she's wrong. Marilyn is special and my mother knows it. I smile at her, nodding in appreciation. The Queen of Cortamagen, Mother of Draglen Descendants, apologizes to a human. WOW! In this moment I know Marilyn is my Wella. Marilyn turns, looking at my mother suspiciously. She relaxes, and the look she gives me is confusing. I hope she's not angry with me.

"Okay, I'll have dinner with you, but only because Showken wants me to. You are not forgiven, yet." Marilyn walks over to my mother's table, reaching out her hand, and Mother shakes it. Shit, I've never seen her shake someone's hand either.

"My son, are you going to stand there with your mouth open, or are you joining us for dinner?" my mother says. I look at Marilyn, glance at my mother, and head towards the table. One of the waiters comes with roast lamb with berries, placing it on the table. Marilyn is impressed, I can tell.

"Thank you, Mother, for the wonderful dinner that is coming, I see all your care in each dish," I say, nodding in appreciation. Our wine is poured, and I notice Marilyn is quiet. I can't stop looking at her, she's so beautiful. I love the frown and uncertainty she's displaying. "Beautiful, the food is going to be fantastic, just wait," I say, leaning over to kiss her cheek. Ohh, she likes my touch. The heat rises to her face, showing her attraction to me. "You look very, very nice, Marilyn, and I can't wait for dessert," I say, smiling.

"Thank you, Showken. The food smells very good," she says, sipping her wine. I look at my mother, who is smiling at me. The other dishes arrive. The appetizers are displayed near our main course, as in my land that is the way it's done; all food out at the same time.

"Well, I don't like this silence. Marilyn, what are your feelings toward my son? Before you answer, I have no need to know your past, how much you're worth, or even who your parents are. I need to know if you plan on staying with my son or breaking his heart," my mother says, taking a bite of food.

"Well, umm Mrs. Draglen. To be honest, I'm not sure where Showken's and my relationship will go, but whatever direction it goes, I think it's between me and Showken," Marilyn says, eyes focused on my mother. Instead of responding, my mother gives her a nod, Marilyn arches a brow at her, and I feel like a female conversation has just happened, without me included. Oh well, I think how wonderful it would be if I could really show Marilyn my land. I always feel love at home. Just then my cell rings.

"Excuse me, I must take this call," I say, walking away from the table. I hear my native language take over as Draken is on the other end. When I'm away far enough that Marilyn can't hear, I speak frankly.

"Yes, brother, what is it?" I ask, chuckling. Draken thinks this is very funny.

"So, you brought a human to our land, and she's eating with Mother," he chuckles. "Can Princess and I come join the dinner? I have to see the woman that's tamed you up close." He laughs again.

"Draken, you are really pushing it, and no, you had better not show up at dinner. Besides, I'm not tamed," I say, looking around to see if I can see Draken, he wants to see her up close, which means he's near. He's annoying at times, and this is one of them. Ah, I see him. Though Marilyn sees just a restaurant, actually it's a small part of Cortamagen. Marilyn believes she's in a really nice restaurant, not in my home country. I smile at my brother, and he waves at me. Wow, my brother, the hard rock, no-nonsense

110

brother, just waved at me. Cess is a pretty awesome lady. "You're waving, now," I say, laughing. I would never have thought Draken would be so carefree.

"Yes, I'm waving. Are you laughing at me, brother?" he asks. I can see his grin. I turn and see my mother and Marilyn talking, I had better get back.

"Yes, I'm laughing. We'll talk later, I'm on a date," I say, chuckling as I hang up the cell phone. I walk back over to the table, finding Marilyn smiling. She's blushing. My mother nods for me to sit. I sit down, smiling at the most important women to me. I start eating, and the table is silent now. I guess while I was talking to Draken, Marilyn and Mother had a good talk. Marilyn looks up at me with those beautiful eyes, giving me a smile that says she's fine now. I feel really good. I'll ask her about what she and my mother spoke of. The dinner is going well. Marilyn and my mother embrace. Bruiser comes back from a great run just as we are leaving. I'm sure Draken has given him food. He looks happy too. Finally parking at Marilyn's apartment, I decide to park and talk with her in the car, hoping I will be invited in.

"Well, it went well, I think," I say, hoping to get her talking.

"Mmm, yep," she says. What? She always talks more than this. I frown a little. I hope my mother has not done any more damage.

"Sweetheart, why are you quiet?" I ask, gently tucking her hair behind her ear. She looks down, rubbing her hands on her thighs. She's nervous, why?

"I'm fine, Showken, the dinner turned out great, and I understand your mother's reaction better now that I've talked with her . . . I need some space, though, it's not because of you. I know that's what people say, but really you're perfect in every way. I just need to think, clear my head," she says, not making eye contact.

"I'm not sure about what you and my mother spoke about, but I do know this; I'm not going to let you go. If you think that 'you need space' speech is going to keep me away, you have a lot to learn. Besides, I . . . umm . . . got us some strawberry cupcakes. I noticed you didn't have dessert. I didn't have any either, so hold on," I say, jumping out of the vehicle and walking to the passenger's side. I open the door, waiting for her to look at me. She finally raises her head. She's like a delicate flower. "I'm not going anywhere. You think I'm perfect and I think you're perfect for me. I want you, Marilyn, please take my hand," I say, holding out my hand. "Let's go inside, relax, and eat some dessert, making love after each cupcake. I got a half dozen," I say. She looks up with tears in her eyes. Placing her hand in mine, she gives me a smile, and nods in agreement. I wrap my arms around her waist. I close her door and open the door for Bruiser, picking up the hidden cupcakes I just made appear from the store.

We get to the door and she turns to me and shakes her head, opening the door wide for me to enter. I'm not letting her go.

"Showken, you are one tough guy to get rid of," she says, pulling off her sexy three-inch heels.

"Now, sexy, why would you want to get rid of me? I can be so much fun if you relax," I say, playfully moving my eyebrows up and down.

"I'm going to get comfy, er . . . I guess you can get comfy too, but keep those pants on," she says, walking to her bedroom smiling.

Bruiser sits at my feet. I really like this pet. I place the cupcakes on the table in front of her sofa. Hmmm, 'keep my pants on', she says. I look at Bruiser, who is right on my heels. "Bruiser I think I'm going to take my pants off. Besides, everything will be off soon," I say to my new pet. I pull off my shirt, shoes, socks and pants. Now I'm in my green underwear. I chuckle to myself, underwear is something I only do on earth. At home I can be free, only wearing a pair of slacks. I turn on her television. I'll never understand the fascination of watching a box. I had better find something that my beauty will like. I flip through the channels, wondering where my lady is. I listen closely, hearing her heartbeat tells me she's still alive. I try to focus on what she's doing. I sniff the air, oh! She's horny. I am, too. I find a movie called "Monster-In-Law", this looks like something she would like. She's coming back out of the room, finally. If she thinks that she has calmed her need for me, we will see.

"Ahhh! Showken, you're naked!" she yells. I laugh, and I pull down my boxers letting her see naked. "Ahhh! Put that away . . . now!" she yells again, but this time with more yearning in her voice. Her eyes are all over my body.

"You said I was naked, I just wanted you to see naked, beautiful," I say, blowing her a kiss. "Now, come over here and sit, I'll get the dessert and something to drink," I say, waving my hand in front of the couch for her to take a seat. This is going to be a fun night.

"Well, thanks for clearing that up, smarty. Oh, I've always wanted to see this movie," she says, coming to relax, wearing a pair of shorts and a t-shirt that says 'Fuck You'.

"Beautiful, do you have some wine?" I ask, not smelling or seeing any.

"No, but I think I have some beer."

"Okay, beer and strawberry cupcakes. Great combination," I say, coming back to sit next to her for our night.

"Thanks, Showken . . . for everything."

"Don't thank me, I need to thank you. I never thought I would meet someone who could capture my attention for longer than a night."

"Wow, umm . . . I don't know what to say to that."

"Don't say anything," I say, handing her a cupcake.

"Thank you."

"You're welcome, sexy."

We eat our cupcakes until there's only one left, drinking two beers apiece. She's laughing at this movie. I like seeing her happy. She curls next to me, and drifts off to sleep. I really want to wake her, but I carry her to the bed. She stirs as I drape the covers on top of us.

"Showken, please," she says. I think she is awake, but no, she's in a deep sleep. I smile, thinking of how to wake her up. Hmmm.

"What do you want, beautiful?" I whisper into her ear, softly kissing her neck. She moans, moving towards me. Whoa, I need to wake her up. I get up, and go get the last cupcake. When I come back, she's sliding her hand into her shorts. Fuck, she's starting without me. Moving quickly to the bed, I pull the covers all the way down and climb back in. I lay my hands on her lower belly, and she wakes up looking at me. I smile, looking at her hand in her shorts. She looks down, feeling embarrassed. I smile, pulling her hand out of her shorts. I start licking each finger. I never take my eyes off of her. She tastes delicious.

"Umm."

"Yes."

"I don't think we should."

"Why?" I ask, continuing to kiss and suck her fingers.

"Showken, please, you're torturing me with your mouth."

"Really? Well, I can torture you with this mouth all over your body," I say, pulling at her shorts. She gasps at how fast I get them off her.

"Maybe we should go to sleep."

"Sleep you will get tomorrow morning," I say, reaching for my cupcake. "We had chocolate last time, but I also like strawberry. I think strawberry and Marilyn will be a good combination."

"Ohhh!"

"Spread your legs, beautiful, I'm hungry," I say, watching her reaction. She slowly opens her legs, and her arousal glistens. I turn the cupcake on my hand and slowly lower it to her sex, spreading the frosting on her and moving it up her belly, also. She moans, "Ohhhh!" I like the sound of that. I stuff the now frosting-free cupcake into my mouth, chewing slowly while holding her legs apart. She's squirming now. I lean down, licking frosting off her hot body. She arches towards me, and I feel frosting all over my face. I chuckle, remembering she said she wanted space. No space, my lovely lady, I think to myself. I continue sucking, pulling at her folds covered in strawberry frosting. I can't stop myself, I make sure every piece of frosting is off before I focus on her first release. "Showken, I'm dying, please," Marilyn whines.

"You're not going to die, sweetness," I say, pushing her shirt over her head. She's now totally bare for me. I squeeze her breasts, loving the feel of them. I dip back down to her sex and start on her clitoris. It's not long before she's pulling my hair, hard. Pushing my tongue into her sex, I'm rewarded with her orgasm filling my mouth. She screams very loud. "AHHHHHHHHHHHH!!" I can't wait, holding myself up with my hands beside her hips I lean down to kiss her. I didn't think I could ever feel this good. I'm inside her and my movements are slow. I want to savor every minute of Marilyn.

MARILYN

I can't believe that I have no control. I told myself that sex with Showken could not happen again, yet I feel so good right now with him inside me. After the talk with his mother, while Showken was on the phone, she explained how she had never intended to offend me, that she had never seen Showken so affected by a woman. He is such a caring, gentle, kind, and fine as hell man. I'm surprised he is not married. He's working me over right now. Those soft lips are amazing. I can't believe he caught me masturbating in my sleep. I guess he wants me, too. Being wakened up with strawberry cupcakes is fun. I can't think any more, he is commanding my body. I open my eyes, loving how attentive he is to me. His lips are everywhere, kissing my breasts, lips, neck, shoulders, and even my hips. He wraps my legs around him, thrusting, taking turns going fast and slow. Mmmmm, the squeezing of my hips is very arousing to me. I love to feel his big hands enjoying me as I enjoy him.

"You feel amazing," he whispers. He doesn't stop moving inside me. He puts my legs on top of his shoulders, holding them in place. Oh my, I think I hear a growl.

"Show, show . . . OHHH, SHOOOOWKEN!" I scream. My climax is hard and loud. He finds his release right after me, moaning loudly.

"HMMMMMM!" The sound comes from deep inside him, and I feel my body tremble just hearing it. I love that sound. I did that. I made him growl, made him lose control. This man is so easy to fall for. We rest on my bed, still entwined with each other. He brushes my sweaty hair out of my face.

"You are so beautiful, don't ever be with another man," he says, looking me in the eye. Whoa, I'm not sure what he's thinking about, but that is not a thought of mine.

"Showken, I'm not with another man. I'm with you, what are you talking about?" I rub my hand gently over his face. He catches my hand before I can remove it, and presses a kiss into my palm. His kiss is hot, very hot. My hand now feels very warm, but its a good warmth. I look into his eyes, and there is that deep green again.

"Precious, you are such a jewel, and I don't share, at all. I don't want you with any other man but me. I won't be sorry for anything I do," he says, planting an open-mouthed kiss on me. The kiss is deep, and it lets me know he's serious.

"I'm not that kind of girl, Showken, I don't sleep around if I'm with a guy. Okay?" I say, trying to get as close as possible to him.

"Marilyn, I'm not some guy, I'm your man. I plan on being the last one," he says, holding my chin up to make sure I don't drop my face. I hope he's not talking about marriage. This is moving too fast. I'm not ready for anything that serious. I really like Showken, but love him enough to be his wife? I don't think so. I'm moody, strange, and have tons of baggage from my past. I'm not going to discuss this.

"I see that your heart rate is picking up speed. I guess you understand I want you forever," he says, searching my eyes to get my reaction.

"I'm just excited to be next to you, wrapped in your arms," I say, resting my head on his shoulder. He rolls onto his back with me still in his arms, now I'm lying on top of him.

"Huh, okay, if you say so, but I'm serious. I will do it right, though," he smiles. "Now, can I have more of you, I feel like a caged beast, needing to fly," he says, chuckling. What a strange thing to say, especially when it sounds like what he said in my dream. I feel his erection, and it's hard. Oh, I guess talking is over.

We continue our sex and small talk throughout the night. It is early morning before we decide sleep would be good. When morning comes, I cook breakfast and he leaves, I think going home. Showken is getting real serious, and I'm sure he is talking about marriage. He said numerous times during sex that he wanted me forever. I'm not sure if it was just in the moment, or if he meant it. This is my last day off work. I go back tomorrow, so I need to get as much rest as possible. I need to go back to bed. Showken didn't give me any sleep last night, and I slept almost an hour this morning. He's like the energizer bunny; he never stops. I'm glad he gave me my bath this morning, I know my ass would have hit the floor if it wasn't for the care he showed me. I pick up my cell heading back to bed, noticing that Jazz called four times and there are six text messages, I'm sure all from her. I'll call her later; I need sleep. I climb into my bed, smelling Showken everywhere. He's in my sheets, pillows, Bruiser even smells like him. Showken is taking over my life. I can't let this happen, I need to get back in control. The sex is good, but marriage . . . commitment is not something I want right now.

***

When I get up five hours later, my attention is called to Bruiser needing to go outside. He's nudging me, and barking for me to get up.

"Ok, Bruiser. Mommy is tired and needs sleep, but I'm getting up," I say to him. As I'm climbing out of bed he heads for the door. I laugh at how wonderful he is to me. Bruiser is my commitment, and he only wants to be fed, patted and walked.

Showken wants way more than I can give. I slip on a pair of jeans, put on my bra and tank top, and pick up my keys to take Bruiser for a walk. My cell phone rings as soon as I'm out the door. I smile, seeing Jazz's name come up.

"Hello, pesty," I say laughing.

"Oh no, don't pesty me," she says, sounding a little annoyed. "You know I want to know the details of his momma, plus I'm assuming he stayed the night since my bestie could only now answer my calls or texts. So spill."

"Well, his mother insulted me at first."

"That bitch! Keep going, I hope you handed her ass to her on a platter."

"Oh, I made it clear that she was not to speak to me the way she did. Then I was going to leave, but she apologized and basically begged me to stay for dinner. Speaking of dinner, he took me to the most magical restaurant ever. I mean, it seems normal on the outside, but Jazz, it's like being outside in the world's best garden," I say, remembering the beauty of this place.

"Really, what's the name? I've never heard of a place like this."

"I'm not sure, but we have to go, even Bruiser was allowed to go, granted Showken owns the place and it was just us inside, but that's still awesome. I could bring my other bestie, Bruiser was able to run free."

"Okay, great, but I want to know more about the momma bitch. Do you think she likes you?"

"At first I thought she hated me, but then Showken had a phone call, leaving me at the table with her. She starts telling me how much she loves her children, and how it was shocking to see Showken fall so deep, this fast. Then she said that she welcomed me into the family. Freaked me out!"

"Hot shit balls! So you're in there, girl! Don't forget me. I want to live good, too."

"First off- wait, hold on a second," I say, trying to get Bruiser's leash under control. He loves the outdoors. "Ok, I'm back. Now I could never forget you, but I'm not going anywhere."

"Mari, this a good guy, who's loaded. Don't start any shit about not being ready. There's no 'I' in team. You getting with this guy is helpful for me."

"Jasmine Halon, I'm not going to be with someone for the team. Besides, I really don't know him and neither do you, so remember whose team you're on, and that's mine. Now, how's Rachel?"

"Fine. Well, he obviously stayed the night, so spill. Is it still good?"

I smile, remembering my night with Showken. "It was awesome. Hey, I'll call you later- I'm back inside now and I need to eat some food. Plus, Bruiser is hungry, too."

"Okay, call me later. Rachel and I might drop by."

"Okay, bring some beer. All of mine is gone, and I'm not getting dressed today," I say, hanging up the phone.

I laugh, knowing Jazz is itching to know more details of

Showken's and my night together. I'm not sure how to explain the cupcake thing, or if I even want to. I don't think I will ever be able to eat cupcakes again without thinking of Showken and his creative ways to eat. I look at the clock on the wall, noticing it's just after 2:00pm. I have the entire day to myself. What is a girl to do?

SHOWKEN

I can't seem to get any work done. I'm thinking about Marilyn every minute, yet still I try to work. I'm drowning myself in paperwork, looking over numbers on our investments. I asked not to be disturbed, so it's shocking that my door opens without a knock. I look up, seeing that it's my brother, the one who doesn't usually come to earth. He doesn't even like the smell, he says. He walks towards me and he doesn't let his eyes leave mine. Why is he here?

"Warton, why are you here?" I snap. He nods.

"I'm here because our mother sent me," he says, calmly. He's very composed when he talks, never raising his voice. That voice may sound calm, but he's always on fire. He is the only brother who settles disputes with fighting, whether in human form or dragon. He is possibly the most dangerous of us all.

"I don't need you here, so leave," I say, growling very low. He growls back. Warton is not used to this land.

"As much as I would like to leave this smelly land, I can't. My job is to keep you in line," he says, calmly.

"FUCK YOU! I don't need watching!" I yell. Realizing I'm at work, I try to lower my voice.

"Showken, I'm here because your beast sometimes gets out of control, especially now that lovely Marilyn is around," he says, sitting down in my chair by the window. Warton is a great warrior, and if I'm in a fight I want him on my side always, but I will not have him here.

"My beast wants out now, to fucking burn your ass back home," I say, feeling my eyes change. I'm really pissed right now. I thought Mother trusted me, but instead she has sent the brother whose only solution is to fight and kill.

"Well, tell your beast to stay put, or else." I can't believe she has done this to me. I can't ask why and risk her getting upset.

"My beast has a mind of its own," I snap. The door opens again and Domlen, Hawken and Layern are all in my office. They stand at the door. Warton and I are face to face.

"You need to calm down, brother. I'm not here to fight, but if you press me . . . well that's a different story," he says, his eyes changing from crystal clear to jet black. I'm not afraid of his beast, but obviously Mother is afraid of what mine can do, and Warton should have that fear, too.

"Showken, stay calm." Domlen says. "We are not at home, but at the family business. Warton, let me show you the office where you will work. You may be here to watch Showken, but you will pull your weight with work. I'll make sure that you do." He is looking at everyone in the room, his eyes constantly moving. I take a step back from Warton. He walks over to Domlen, and they give each other a nod and leave the room. I'm pacing back and forth. I can't have Warton here.

"Showken."

"Hawken, Layern, you both need to get to work," I say, going back to my desk and taking a seat. They both leave, shrugging. I sit in my office alone. If my mother sent Warton, she's concerned, but why? I'm not going to do anything dangerous. I just want to be with Marilyn, that is all. The day is soon over. I'm driving home when I feel the need to talk with Marilyn. I voice-command my cell to dial her number. She picks up after three rings.

"Beautiful, how's your day been?"

"Oh, it's been lazy."

"Really, can I come over?" I need to be with her. I miss her

"Ah, Jasmine and Rachel are coming over. Besides, I'm sore," she giggles. I smile, too.

"I've got a remedy for that soreness, I can come when they leave, or if you're not ashamed of me, I could visit with your friend."

"What? Why? I mean, you want to hang out with my friend and her kid? Really?"

"Do you love them?"

"Yes, but-"

"No buts, if you love them, so do I. I would love to get to know them better, since I already love them." It's silent on the phone. Please Marilyn, I need you tonight, I beg in my head.

"Okay, but bring something to eat, Jasmine is bringing the beer."

"I can do that."

"Food, not cupcakes."

"I will bring food, too," I smile, hearing her laughter. We are both sharing this laugh, and I feel better already, despite being watched by Warton.

***

I decide to make a dish to bring over to Marilyn's house tonight. I've avoided my brothers; I'm not pleased that Warton is here. After taking a shower and changing into a pair of shorts and a jersey, I head to the kitchen to cook a meal, something quick. Spaghetti should do, with garlic bread. I leave for Marilyn's place in no time. When I pull up to her apartment, I sit and listen to Jasmine and her talk, using my powerful hearing. I can hear their laughter. I hear Marilyn tell Jasmine that she can't be with me. How she's not fit for my world. I shake my head with a smile, if she only knew that she's perfect for my world. Her personality is just what I need. I gather up the food and walk to the door, giving it two loud knocks. I hear Marilyn's heartbeat pick up pace. Good. She finally opens the door.

"Hi, beautiful."

"Hello"

"You going to invite me in?"

"Oh, yes, come in, Showken."

"Thanks," I say, as I step in the door. I lean over and kiss her cheek. Jasmine's eyes are like bright lights, all wide and shiny from excitement about Marilyn and me. I set the food on her counter in the kitchen, making sure I place some cupcakes on the counter. I turn and see Marilyn, eyes are wide. Yes, sweetheart, I brought us some cupcakes, but I have our own box, I think, looking into her eyes. I hold up the second box, placing it in the fridge. I hear the gasp. "Huh!" I wink at her. Bruiser is right by my leg in no time, my new pet.

"Hey Bruiser, you watching these ladies for me?" I ask, rubbing him. We play for a minute. I head over to Jasmine who is watching me, giving me a smile of satisfaction.

"Hello Jasmine."

"You can call me Jazz, and this little one here is my daughter, Rachel," she says, pointing to the Young playing with some dolls. The Young looks up at me, granting me a beautiful smile.

"Okay Jazz, very beautiful daughter you have. I hope you like spaghetti, garlic bread and cupcakes."

"I want a cupcake, mommy," the Young says.

"You have to eat your food first, baby girl," Jazz says. Marilyn is still standing at the door, watching me. She must not have believed me when I said I loved her.

"Precious, you okay?" I ask, walking up to her. I stop a few feet away, smiling. I see she's wet in her private, slowly getting soaked, like poured honey. Later baby, I promise, I say in my head, looking her in the eyes. I hold out my hand for her. She stands there a second.

"I'm fine, just fine, Showken. Thanks for dinner, it smells great," she says, ignoring my hand. I chuckle. She's nervous now. She walks over to the cabinet and pulls out some plates. She doesn't have a real table, it's very tiny, so I guess we are all eating in her living area. I go over and start fixing plates with her. Jazz gets her Young ready for dinner, taking her to wash her hands in the bathroom. I have a chance to speak with her alone.

"Love, just relax, we're going to have a good time," I say, standing behind her. I pull her hair over her shoulder, softly kissing her neck. Her body stiffens with my touch. I like that.

"I told you, I'm fine, Showken," Marilyn says. I'm not convinced, but I will leave this subject for later. Jazz and her Young come back and we fix everyone plates. The Young has this little chair at the coffee table. I make sure Bruiser has something to eat, and I sit on the floor, letting the women have the sofa. We end up watching a Disney movie because of the Young. She selects "The Little Mermaid". This movie is fascinating. I can't believe they let this Young believe that mermaids are like this. The mermaids I encounter are quite dangerous creatures. I've kissed a few, but I've killed more. Oh well. We laugh and play games after the Young falls asleep. The last game we decide to play is Truth or Dare. It's Jazz's idea.

"Marilyn, truth or dare?" I ask. She looks at me then Jazz. These ladies are getting to their limit on drinks, oh well. I'll call for a driver for Jazz and her Young, she can't drive home like this.

"No, Showken, it's my turn again, you have not answered any questions or done as many dares as Jazz and I. Nope, it's your turn," Marilyn says, giggling. Oh, she's paying attention. I have avoided my turn numerous times. I can't answer the questions they keep asking.

"Well, personally, I'd like to know if Showken has a brother who would be interested in me. Just for fun, nothing serious," Jazz says, taking a swallow from her beer. She's serious. Oh Jazz, you just don't know what you're asking.

"Nah, Jazz, stop distracting him with 'lets hook Jazz up', I want some questions, I mean, answers from Showken," Marilyn slurs.

"I think I'll make you both some coffee," I say, rising from the floor.

"Oh, no you don't! I don't need any coffee. Do you need coffee, Jazz?"

"Nope, I feel good." They both look at me with their brows lifted. Okay, if they want me to play, I'll play.

"Okay, what do you want to know?" I ask, smiling.

"I'm first," Marilyn says. I lick my lips, sit back on the floor and give them both a huge grin.

"Well, baby, what do you want to know?" I say, giving Marilyn my full attention. Her heart speeds up, and I can almost taste her arousal it's so strong.

"Umm, how many women you've slept with?" I can't take my eyes off her. She looks beautiful, but here goes the start of my lies. The list of women goes back more than a couple of centuries. Shit, I don't like this, but I'll try to tell part of the truth.

"First I need for you to understand, women have always been a weakness of mine, and I never thought I would love someone. I've slept with many since I started working the family business, which is about fifty," I say, reading her reaction. She looks at me, takes a deep breath and relaxes. I catch Jazz mouthing the word "man-whore". I just stare at Marilyn. There have been more women than that. I just gave her the ones I've actually fallen asleep with since I've been working for the business.

"Okay, did you use them?"

"I did, but they used me, too."

"What number am I?"

"I'm not playing this anymore, if you want to know more about me, beautiful, it will be when we are alone." I can tell she's angry. Why did she ask that question, shit? I didn't even tell her the truth. Women are so confusing.

"Jazz is my family. Whatever you say, you can say in front of her," she glares. I put my hands together, because she looks so hot being angry at me. I could strip her right here and now. I don't say anything. I hear her breathing picking up. I won't take my eyes off her. I release a scent to put only Jazz asleep. She immediately starts yawning.

"I'm getting sleepy. I better get going."

"There is a car waiting for you, Jazz. I don't want you driving with the child."

"Ok, thanks," Jazz says. She gathers her things, picks up the Young and gives Marilyn a kiss on the cheek. Marilyn doesn't move. I let Jazz out of the apartment and watch her to the limo that's waiting for her. When she's safely inside, I close the door and turn and see Marilyn looking at me, with hurt in her eyes. I walk right over to her and kneel before her.

"Showken, just tell me what number I am."

"You're not a number, you're the only one. Please don't get angry about something you asked."

"No, I'm not the only one, when you get bored you will leave me, too. I'll be a number sooner or later," she takes a breath. "I think we should end this before someone gets hurt, which will be me."

"No, there is no going back, no ending. I love you and you love me. Tell me, please. Let me hear it from your lips."

"I can't, Showken, fifty women is a lot to take in. Yet, I can't really judge. I have a past, and I promise when you find out, this will end. I rather we do this now." I hear what she's saying, but I don't care about her past, mine will always be worse than hers. I walk over to the stereo and put in a CD that says 'slow music'. The music starts playing. I walk towards her, she stands and before she can think I have her in my arms dancing.

"I can't dance, Showken."

"Yes you can, baby," I say, swiftly bending and placing her legs around my waist. "Now just move the top of your body," I say. I start dancing her around, grinding my body all over her. I love her; she's not ending anything.

"Please, baby, tell me," I plead, moving her up against the wall to her bedroom door.

"Showken, I-"

"Please, I love you Marilyn, tell me now."

"I, I, what does it matter?"

"It matters, Love. Trust me." I move my hands up her shirt, needing to feel her skin. She moans as my thumbs softly circle her nipples. Oh, mmm, I love this woman. I won't lose her.

"Yes."

"Yes what, say it baby."

"I."

"Please I need to hear it." She hesitates, looking me in the eyes.

"I LOVE YOU!" she yells. I growl and head for her bed. I can't control myself. I'm tearing her clothes off. I keep my mouth busy on her lips, neck and shoulders so she doesn't notice the rips in her pants or shirt. I feel her pull my hair hard. I'm spreading her legs fast. I smell her arousal through her panties, I thought the scent was strong earlier, but now I think I don't ever want to leave this room. I bend down, using my teeth to tear at her bra. I can't even slow down to do all of the things I should. I'm in her face in no time. I look her in the eyes as I push myself inside her sweet body. "Ahhhhhh!" she cries out.

"I love you," I whisper in her ear, continuing to make slow love to her.

MARILYN

My walls are crumbling. I didn't plan on sleeping with Showken again. I just said 'I love you' to him. Well, I actually yelled it, but he said it back. He's going to hate me when he finds out I was nothing but a whore. I'm trying to think of how to stop this, but he feels so good. My body loves his hands all over me. Our chests, touching, feel so right.

"You are perfect for me, beautiful," he says, softly biting my ear. I can't control the moan. "Mmmm," my body responds to him. I'm not even sure what he and I are. Is he my boyfriend? I'm not sure. Showken entwines our hands, squeezing just enough to make my body shiver. The rhythm of his thrusting inside me is amazing.

I feel like he's taking me to the clouds with each push.

"More," I moan.

"Okay," Showken says, low. He rises just a little. He is now staring into my eyes. I can't keep staring at him and I close my eyes, enjoying our bodies connecting. I feel his head lean down over my breasts, he captures me with his mouth, biting softly, sending me over the edge. "OHHHHH!" I yell.

"Yes, beautiful," he continues. "I love that you scream in ecstasy because of me."

"You feel, feel, oh, Showken, please don't stop."

"Never," he says, releasing our hands to squeeze my breasts. This man is amazing. Maybe I should stop fighting, "Ohh, Showken?" I pant.

"You like that, huh?"

"Yes, Ohh!"

"Mmmm, don't hold back, go on, scream, Precious."

"OOOOKKKKAAAYYY!!"

Showken finds his release soon after me. He flips us over quickly, now I'm lying on top of him. Trying to catch my breath, I notice how hot it is. I know I have the air conditioner on. Everyone knows that when you live in Paradise Valley, Arizona, the air conditioner has to stay on most of the year. I rub my hand back and forth on Showken's chest, and feel the heat radiating off his body. Shit, he has a fever.

"Hey, you have a fever. Why didn't you stay at home instead of spreading your germs? I can't get sick, I have bills to pay, which require me working.'"

"Aww, you worried about me? Thanks love, but I don't have a fever."

"Umm, yes you do," I say, lifting my body off him. "I can feel the heat all over you. I should have noticed this before sleeping with you. I need to make myself some green tea. I hear it can sometimes prevent colds." I slide next to him, and he watches my every move.

"I'm not sick, beautiful, just . . . happy," he says, in deep thought.

"Don't try to be tough, if you're sick I'll make you some soup, but you can't sleep in my bed. I have to work, sick is not something I can afford."

"I'm not sick, now stop all this talk about your bills, work, and soup. I can pay your bills if that's what troubles you." He looks healthy, but his body is on fire. He's taking some Tylenol regardless. I'm not taking any money from him; I pay my own way. Besides, the men I've encountered always want something in return from me.

"I don't want your money. That is never up for discussion, I will work and pay my own bills. Now, I'm no doctor, but I know a fever when I feel one. I'm going to my medicine cabinet in the bathroom and getting you some Tylenol. Before you say anything, that's not up for discussion either." He gives me a huge smile and those dimples make me want to just bite him. Damn, he's fine. He licks his lips and stares at me for a few seconds.

"Listen, sometimes my body can get hot," Showken says. "I'm pleased to see you caring about me like this, but I'm not taking any Tylenol. Now as for me paying your bills, don't close a conversation before it starts," he continues. "I want to spend more time with you, I want to hear you say 'I love you, Showken' not only when we are having sex. I need you around more, not working two jobs; we need to see each other often. I can relax and spend more time with you, as it's a family business, my brothers can handle it."

"What are you saying, Showken?" I say, suspicious.

"I want to take care of you, spend time with you, and maybe take you to my land."

"Showken, wait... this, us, we are not even supposed to be in bed together. I didn't mean for this to happen. I really like you, but be honest, this between us will never work." I take a deep breath. "We should not make plans to spend more time together. I think that after this night, lets go our separate ways, okay."

"You really think I will walk away from you. Love, I'm not your average guy, I will spend time with you. You want me as much as I want you. Don't you want to know me better? I could be a monster," he says, smiling. Though he's smiling, there is something that looks like fear in his eyes. He can't want me that bad, he just told me about all of his women, besides, my past is not something he would like.

"You hungry?" he asks

"Umm, no, it's late. I try not to eat late, it's not good for you."

"Well, I'm going to raid your fridge." Hold up, he's got my mind sidetracked. I just said we should not see each other, and he talking about spending more time together.

"Showken, wait. I don't think you understand. I'm not asking for this to end. I'm telling you it will end." Showken climbs out of the bed, showing me his entire body. I don't ever think I've seen him in his entirety long enough to admire this unbelievable man in front of me. His body is ripped. There is not one piece of fat on him. His arms are huge, those abs look delicious and his legs have muscles everywhere. He must work out every day. I finally bring my eyes up to his, and he is smiling again.

"Do you like?"

"Yeah, but it won't stop my decision, no matter what."

"I'm going for food, be ready for round two," he says, walking out of the room. He is stubborn. I mean this must be a pride thing, why would he want me? I keep telling him to leave me alone, yet he still insists he wants to spend more time with me. I'm not sure if I want to spend more time. That could lead to him asking about my past, and I don't want to explain anything to him. He wouldn't understand that selling my body for money was all I could do to eat every day. I have been on drugs, taking anything and everything to avoid thinking about what I was doing. I've been clean for four years now. I'm not really supposed to drink, but I never was an alcoholic, everything else, that's another story. I am listening to see if he's coming back when I smell food. Is he cooking? He really is hungry, shit. I try to think what he could be cooking; everything was frozen, except some T.V. dinners and some lunchmeat in the fridge. I smell food cooking. I sit for a minute, realizing that it sounds like he's frying something.

"SHOWKEN!" I yell. He is at the door within seconds; damn he can run. "What are you doing in my kitchen? It smells and sounds like you are frying food. I thought there was food left over?"

"There was some food left over, but I ate that while I was taking out the hamburger meat to make some burgers. I made you one, too. You'll need your energy," he says, grinning wickedly.

"How is the meat thawed that quick?"

"I have my ways, besides you know I'm a hot guy," he says, laughing. He turns and goes back into the kitchen. Then I hear his voice by my ear, 'round two, Love'. I rub my ear, looking around the room; he's not in here, but I'm sure I just heard his voice next to my ear, I almost want to say I could feel his breath on me. I yell for him. He comes to the door like he's been there the entire time.

"Showken, did you . . . never mind." I'm going to sound like a lunatic. I knew all those drugs would catch up with me one day, never thought it would start now.

"Did I what, sweetie?"

"Never mind, my mind is damaged some. I think sleep is calling me," I say, slowly. I must need sleep. I know I heard him at my ear.

"Yes, get some rest. I'll be back in one hour, with dessert," he says, leaving me to think of his hot body and cupcakes. I get comfy and drift off to sleep.

***

I don't hear him come into the room, but I feel his body pushed up against my back. He wakes me with gentle kisses on my back and shoulder.

"Hey, beautiful, I want to talk with you before dessert," he says, laying his head on my shoulder as he hugs me tight. I'm a little nervous about talking. I glance at the clock on my dresser and see it's after 2 a.m. I try to turn to face him, but he holds me still.

"There are things about me I can't tell you right now. I will tell you, though, I promise. I just want you to know I'm not perfect." I lie there absorbing what he just said. Showken has some secrets and they must be really deep, but why tell me? Oh, I almost forgot, he doesn't accept we are not getting together.

"What things?"

"Things that you wouldn't believe," he breathes into my hair, and I feel his body getting warmer.

"Showken, nothing you say will shock me."

"Yes, there are some things that will shock you, but I'm not giving you up. I will tell you later. Now, I have dessert for you," he says, and I feel the smile on my back. I can't help but smile, too. I'm tired, but he's not taking no for answer on anything right now.

"I'm not hungry, remember?"

"I know you're not, but I am," he says, reaching behind his

back, I hear him pick something up. He brings his arm back around me and sets down a box of red velvet cupcakes. Oh, this is going to be a long night. I will enjoy it, because come tomorrow I will end this before I get hurt.

"You only have two choices, baby," Showken says, flipping me onto my back. I gasp at how fast he moves me. I can't help feeling butterflies. He slides his body over mine, only to rise straddling my hips. He is so close that I feel the heat from his skin all along my body, but we are joined only at the axis. I can feel his erection bumping against my pelvis. He picks up two cupcakes. "Soft or rough?"

This is exciting.

"Ummm . . . " I can't decide. "Rough," I say. He immediately smears both cupcakes roughly over my breasts, belly, hips and my sex, licking each finger after he's done. Now I'm covered in red velvet cupcakes.

"Time to eat," he grins.

***

I'm sore. It's morning, and I should be up, getting ready for work. Yet I'm in bed with Showken, with a sore body. He is not allowed to bring any cupcakes to my home again. Wait, there will not be any more over-nighters. I need to get up and get ready for work. I shake Showken a little to wake him, he needs to go home, work, or something, he just has to leave here.

"Baby, go back to sleep, you need to rest," he says, moving closer. I didn't think we could get that close, but he has found a way to have our legs and bodies touching. I'm really going to miss this.

"I have to work, and you have to leave," I say. I feel soft kisses on my shoulder, God I'm going to miss this.

"Oh, I called and made arrangements for you at work, both jobs. So lets sleep or… "

"What do you mean you made arrangements? I can't miss days just because, my rent will be due soon!" I snap. I can't believe he called my jobs. I'm not a little girl, if I wanted the day off I know how to take a day off. He will not control my life.

"Showken, you can't-"

He cuts me off, "I can, I want to get to know you better, and you were all about working today, so I fixed it. Don't worry, you will still get paid. I just want you to come over to my home, and we can have a day of you and me," he says. Damn, he has a sexy voice.

"How did you convince my boss to give me a day off? He's liable to hire a new waitress. I'm sure my other job has fired me by now . . . Showken, you are not good for me, I need to work and you need to run a business."

"I need to have morning sex, shower sex and then we go out for breakfast and have a day of fun. As for how I got the day off, when I said I called, I did call, my brother Domlen, and he can be very convincing."

I just lie there and think. It's like a losing battle with Showken, he never gives up.

"Showken, I-"

"No. Sex, more sex, day of fun," he says, chuckling. He pins me down and is on top of me, rubbing his body on mine.

"Showken!" I yell, smiling.

"You know you want it."

"Well, maybe your idea sounds good but-"

"No buts either, unless we are talking about your round, firm, and sweet, I might add, buttocks." I laugh, shaking my head in disbelief. Why can't I say no? Oh, yeah, I love him. I've got to get myself out of this situation. It doesn't look like it's going to happen today.

"Fine, I will spend the day with you, but so help me Showken, if I'm fired tomorrow I'm going to kick your ass," I say, raising a brow. He chuckles, leaning down over me. He tricks me, I think he's going to kiss me on the lips, but no. He tilts his head, leans in closer and sticks his tongue in my ear, causing me to scream. I feel warm everywhere now. "Mmmm," I moan. I guess this is round one. This is going to be the last day together. It has to be, who wants a whore like me.

SHOWKEN

I owe Domlen. He really came through for me. I originally asked Layern, but he was occupied with some women. I'm glad my brother is back from his lonely state. Marilyn and I had a great morning, and I want to have a fun day with her. I've arranged for us to go hiking and have a private lunch and a helicopter ride. I hope this all goes as planned. I need to stop by the house first and see my brothers, with Warton here there is no telling what could happen. I have Marilyn and Bruiser in my Hummer, and that's all that matters. I glance over and see her staring out of the window. I know she has doubts about us, but she's my Wella, I just have to convince her. I'm not used to this, women fall at my feet, literally. This convincing her is tiring, but she's worth it.

"Beautiful," I say. "We are going to stop at my house first, I have to pick up some things for our day." I can't stop staring at her. If I were human all the way, not paying attention to the road could be fatal, but my beast can watch for me.

"Hey, keep your eyes on the road. Besides, when are you going to tell me where we are going?"

"Surprise means not knowing, love. Patience, we must work on that, I can help in that area."

"Oh no, you are not teaching me patience, ever. I might lose my mind." She smiles and I want her now. We finally make it to my home.

***

"Why don't you and Marilyn stay for an early lunch?" Hawken asks. I'm not sure what's going on, but my brothers know that I'm going to be gone all day. I'm not eating with them. We are barely in the door. Marilyn looks at me. I don't want to be here. Besides, Warton is here to watch me, so I'm definitely not staying.

"Sorry brother, we have plans," I say, calmly. I try to go around him, and he makes a point of getting in my way. We stare at each other for a few seconds.

"Hey, I'm not sure what's going on, but I think you boys should calm down," Marilyn says, getting between us. "I can feel tension between you two." I really could punch Hawken, he is the delivery service of bad news. I hear Domlen coming, shit.

"Hey brother, early lunch won't hurt, it's already prepared," Domlen says, turning towards Marilyn. "There are no boys in this house, watch your words," he says. He looks at me, and he must see the anger on my face. I'm going to rip his head off.

"Domlen, don't. My lady, not yours," I say, glaring.

I glance at Marilyn, who looks nervous now. I take her hand and push through Hawken, walking her to my room. Once inside, I breathe a sigh of relief. I shield the door using one of my powers, making it impossible for my brothers to come inside.

"Are you okay, precious?" I ask, walking towards her. She's standing, looking around like she's never been in here.

"Yes, I'm fine . . . I think I should go to work. Your brothers, I don't think they like me. I think it's best if I go." I stop walking just a couple of feet in front of her. After all I've told her, she still thinks I will let her go.

"No, my brothers are fine with you, it's me they have a problem with," I say, walking closer to her again. "I want you badly right now, we have a whole day together." The knock on the door interrupts my thoughts. Layern. I go and open the door.

"What?"

"Stay, just to eat a little." He looks at me, and then gives Marilyn a huge smile. "Hello Marilyn, it's nice to see you again. I promise my brothers and I will be on our best behavior. I just told Domlen he owes you an apology. So, will you stay to eat with us?" Layern is back. I do believe he's flirting with Marilyn. I give him a low growl and his eyes are now on me. I'm not Draken, nobody could be that jealous, but I'm not that far away. I'm a dragon first, and it's my nature to protect what's mine. Dragons are possessive naturally, but we are Draglen descendants, and our blood drips with jealousy.

"Yes, we will stay and eat. Bruiser will need a bowl of water." What? I can't believe her. She was just saying she should leave; now she wants to stay. She's up to something. Marilyn, you don't know what you've just committed us to.

"I'll see you both in a few," Layern says. "Oh, Marilyn, my brothers and I always love a beautiful woman to grace our table. Bruiser will be taken care of also." He walks away. Closing the door, I turn towards her and she sits down on my bed. What is she thinking?

"Baby, what are you trying to do? My brothers are . . . different. We should get our backpacks and go. I'll make sure we have lunch," I say, hoping. I don't want to eat with them right now; I really want to know more about Marilyn. Besides, she's going to have to find out the truth soon. I want her, and need to claim what's mine.

"Showken, your brothers are determined to get us to stay, I'm not sure why, but I want to know. Maybe they know something about you that I should know," she says, tilting her head. Does she think- wait, she thinks my brothers have her best interest at heart. Oh Marilyn, I'm the only one you can trust right now.

"They know something," I murmur.

"What was that?"

"What are you talking about? Listen if you want to stay, okay, we will stay, but you stay close to me, it's for your own good."

"You will be surprised at how I can handle myself, especially with men. I didn't forget to bring protection."

"Oh yes, your gun. Well, that's no good. Forget it. Come, let's eat." I move really close to her, looking into those beautiful grey eyes. I need a kiss now, but if I start, we won't leave this room for the rest of the day. I guide her to the eating area, noticing she's looking around the room. Ah, the white room, my brothers and I don't think much about it. However, a stranger will be confused to see all men in a home with an all white room for eating. It was our mother's idea, a way to be reminded of where we come from. In Cortamagen, white is the symbol of our people and our land. So, eating in this room is like eating at home. Everyone else sees white, but we see colors, flowers, fruit and gardens, our home. My brothers are standing, waiting for Marilyn to be seated. I see Warton looking at me. I would have preferred Brumen, but Warton I can see now is going to test me.

We walk to the table, and after Marilyn is seated, we all sit. The table is filled with food: breads, fruit, meats of all kinds, wine, and desserts.

"Whoa, Showken, you guys eat like this every day?" she asks.

"Yes, baby. We eat like this, and usually it's more." I lean down and kiss her forehead. She smells so good.

"Well, Marilyn, tell me about the girl who's stolen the player, Showken," Warton says, smiling. I'm going to kill him.

"Warton, if you want to remain intact, don't start anything," I growl, uncontrollably. This is not going to go well.

"It's okay, Showken. Remember, you told me fifty women," Marilyn says, irritated. I told her nobody makes me feel like her, yet I still feel her anger.

"Ha, fifty! Showken, if you are going to tell her secrets, why don't you tell her who you really are," Warton says.

"Shut up, before I make you," I snap.

"Showken, you do know that she has to know sooner or later," Hawken says. This is why they wanted us to stay, to trap me. Well fuck them, I'm leaving.

"Baby, lets go," I say, standing. "I'll make sure you eat." When I reach for her hand, she snatches away. I smile at her and she's pissed, cute, but we are leaving.

"What other secrets, Showken?" She folds her arms across her chest. Wow, she's going to take a stand, I guess.

"Marilyn, we need to go. I will tell you everything, just not here." I pull her hand for her to stand, and she snatches it back.

"Showken, tell her, or I will, that is my other reason for being here. Mother says to make sure you come clean with this human," Warton says.

"Yes, you need to tell her, Showken. You're too close to her and she has to know. If you don't want her, wipe her memory and let her go," Hawken says, standing. Layern and Domlen are still seated, but I see their guards are up. I can't believe this. My eyes roam the room as I'm trying to think of what to do. I laugh out loud, because I could literally kill my brothers right now, and I think I'm losing my mind. I move away from the table and begin to pace. I see Marilyn watching me, with a slight fear in her eyes. I don't want her scared of me, but my beast would scare her. Why am I being backed into a corner?

"You're being backed into a corner because you would never have told her in time, and we will leave in a few months," Layern says, tilting his head. I know they are wondering whether or not my beast is itching to get out, and they would be right. I would like to release my beast right now.

"Showken, I'm leaving. I don't have time for you and your crazy brothers. I'm not sure what's going on here, but I'm done. Goodbye," she says standing to leave. Before I can stop, a growl escapes from me. The look on her face is pure fear.

"I think you need to sit down," Domlen says, commanding. Marilyn looks around, and all eyes are on her. Shit, fuck it. I will deal with this head on.

"Marilyn, please sit down, I have something to say," I look at all my brothers, hoping they will leave the room. Wishful thinking, they all stand and I see her in full fear now. She reaches into her purse and pulls out her gun. Big mistake. I see my brothers take offense. Warton uses his powers and the gun is suddenly in his hand. The atmosphere in the room has changed, everyone's beast is on high alert, and I just want to get away. I move quickly over to Marilyn. With no effort I pull her into my arms, pull out my portal and head home to Cortamagen. I hear her screaming and crying as we go through the portal. My beast is trying to get out, to protect her. I know my brothers will follow me. I want to tell her to be calm, and a roar comes from my mouth. It's taking everything inside me to stay in human from. She finally screams until she passes out, just as I appear in my room in the castle. What have I done?

***

She's been asleep for over six hours. I rubbed her down with some of my oils to help calm her, and shielded my room so no one could enter. Being a dragon, if I don't want anyone in then no one comes in. I'll just lie here and wait for her to open her eyes. I need to see those beautiful grey eyes. I should not have brought her here like this. I know she's seen our eyes change and heard my growling. The room became filled with predators and she was the prey. She'll hate me for a little while, but I won't let her go, I love her. There's a knock at the door. I narrow my eyes until I realize who it is. Softly, I move from the bed and walk to the door.

"Hello, Cess. Draken sent you."

"Oh, Showken, I came by to see Marilyn, and to see how you were doing," Cess says softly. She's really beautiful. She has such a loving heart; she will be a great queen someday.

"Thanks, Cess, but I'm not up for company right now. Marilyn is still asleep. I just wanted it to be the two of us when she wakes. Besides, Draken let you come alone?"

"No, he's close I'm sure, but I just wanted to make sure that you know I'm here for you. I wish I could give you a hug right now, but Draken is so jealous."

"Yes, I know, thanks for coming to check on me, Cess. I will be fine as soon as she's awake. I love her and I won't lose her. Hawken and Warton started this. They told her I have secrets I need to come clean with, but I'll get them one day."

"Oh Showken, I can't wait to see you smile again." Cess stops for a minute. "Your brother is getting nervous, I told him if I couldn't come to see you by myself there would be no sex for a week," she laughs.

"I know Draken didn't like that. She's a nice lady, Cess. I hope she still wants me, because I won't let her go."

"It will be fine, and don't be mad at your brothers."

"You mean Draken in particular."

"Yes, you're his favorite, don't push him out, okay?"

"You are so good for him, I'm glad to call you sister. I would only do this for you, Cess," I say, reaching to touch her, I flinch as I hear and feel a growl. My brother is jealous. She leaves and I go back to watching Marilyn. I have clothes and food waiting for her. I need to tell her mind-blowing information. She's my Wella, now I just have to convince her. To pass the time, I get my room in order, and make sure that the bathroom is stocked with products for her. I even have beer in my icebox for her. She's going to hate me, but I had to bring her. This was the safest place I could think of. I hear her moving, she's waking up. I rush to the end of the bed, waiting. She moves around, stretching and yawning. She looks peaceful, calm. Maybe she's okay now. Her eyes roam the room and then they stop at mine. She stares for a second.

"What the fuck are you? And where the fuck am I at?" Well, she's still feisty.

"First, I'm so glad you're awake. I've waiting for over eight hours now. Second, this is my home, my real home. You're in Kalin, Cortamagen. And third, I'm a dragon-shifter." I feel relief telling her. I want her to know- I need her to know, so we can get past the shock and move on. I really miss her body.

"Showken, what happened? I remember being at your house, your brothers were standing, I pulled my gun and . . . Oh SHIT!!" Her breathing is picking up. She's balled herself tightly in my bed. "I want to go home, please don't kill me."

"Beautiful," I say, moving closer. "I wouldn't ever harm you. It's still me, the man you have screamed for; your body yearns for me. I miss you so much, Love. I won't touch you, though. I want you to want me. I want to lick your entire body, twice. Just don't be scared of me."

"Your brothers, are they, umm, dragons, too?"

"Yes, they are dragons, but they wouldn't harm you, they wanted me to be honest with you because I love you." When those words come out of my mouth, I know it's true. My brothers were only trying to help, and though they picked a fucked-up way, they still wanted to help.

"Why did you bring me here? Never mind, only my life would

be this crazy, just take me home," she says. I still sense fear.

"You are fearful of me, precious, please don't be frightened. Everyone in the castle is excited to meet you."

"You're crazy, let me go."

"No, I won't let you go, but you are free to leave the room and walk around. I will accompany you though, dragons are the most dangerous, but we live among other species." I smile, hoping she will relax. I smell her arousal. She's angry, but she still wants me. Yes!

"Other species, what others?"

"Listen, my brother, who is heir to the throne, is married to a human, so don't worry. Whatever else is in our land will never hurt you."

"Heir to a throne, what? Showken, the more you talk the more confused I get."

"I'm a dragon, and I'm part human. The dragon is my natural being, human form is something we choose to have because we like earth for certain things." I put my hands behind my head and just look at her. I can't stay this far away. I vanish, and reappear right next to her. She gasps, and wants to scream, but clasps her hands over her mouth.

"What do you eat? Humans?"

"The myths are outrageous, no. We eat bread, desserts, fruit, meat- of animals, drink wine, really no different than what you eat," I say, reaching to touch her knee, but she moves it.

"Why am I here?" she asks. I can't say because I love you and want you to move here with me forever and become my Wella, my life mate.

"Can I prove some things to you before you make up your mind?"

She looks at me and fuck, her smell hits me. I want to be inside her so bad right now, my body is aching. She looks around the room, and both hands cover her face. This is when Layern's gift would come in handy.

"I want to show you me, my land and anything else you want before you say you don't want me. I want you, Marilyn, so bad, especially now." We stare at each other and the room is filled with her smell. Fuck.

"I guess my choice has been taken from me." She takes a deep breath. "So, are you going to try and convince me sleeping with a dragon is okay?"

"Yes, I am," I give her my huge smile, because when I'm done, she's going to beg me to take her to bed. I climb out of the bed, it's too tempting to be that close. "Would you like a bath? Everything you need is right through that arch, body wash, shampoo, and clothes." She shakes her head yes, and I walk to the archway in the room. I don't have doors inside my room. I want to see everything. She watches me for a second, and then slides out of the bed. She keeps her eyes on me as she walks, turning back around to make sure I'm still standing far enough away from her. She's always trying to get away. I hear the gasp as she walks into my bathroom; it's as big as her entire one bedroom apartment. I chuckle to myself; this is going to be fun. I love this human lady and I want her, I must win her heart soon. I wonder why Mother hasn't called for me. I wouldn't leave Marilyn, anyway. Besides, when I see Hawken and Warton, blood will be shed.

MARILYN

Things just never go right for me. Instead of just meeting a really good guy, I meet a crazy lunatic. He's something, not sure if he's a dragon, he's in human form. Dragons are not humans, he's something though. I stopped drugs long ago, but he took me somewhere traveling very fast in a very small space. Showken looks amazing, and one thing is for sure: he's a rich son of a bitch. This bathroom is beyond amazing, all decked out in different greens. It reminds me of the different shades his eyes can be. I need to get to a phone and call the police. I know he might talk his way out of jail, but at least Jazz would come save me. I walk over to a huge counter, there are soaps, towels and perfume. He's taken care of everything. I turn to start the water, noticing Showken in the room with me.

"I don't need your help," I snap.

"I know, just making sure everything is okay."

"Listen, kidnapper, and umm, what did you say? Dragon. Well listen, I don't believe in dragons and if I did, you look nothing like a dragon." I glare at him. I'm so angry with him right now, but my body is a traitor and melts every time he smiles. I will not be sidetracked. I'm being held hostage.

"Wait, where did you take me? I need to know as much information as possible so I can say how I went crazy and met a guy who claims to be a dragon," I chuckle. "I'm going fucking nuts, a dragon! Yeah right Showken, you are going to wherever you want in the tin city, better known as prison."

"Not in your wildest dream, beautiful. I'm not going to jail, and yes, I'm a real dragon. I will show you my land after you bathe and dress, and if you're nice, my dragon, too." He looks serious, almost convincing. I hope he's just crazy and not killer crazy.

"I'm free to leave after I dress?"

"Yes, but only with me. In my land you will always be unsafe until you are my Wel- . . . umm, I will be waiting for you." He almost said something. I wonder what it was. Anyways, I will take my bath and wait until I have a chance to escape from him. All I know is that he and his brothers are weird and have crazy eyes and stupid growls. Growls, who does that? No, there are no such things as dragons, are there? I get undressed right by this gigantic bath that is a baby pool. Jazz would love this place. He is a very rich kidnapper. I climb in and my body relaxes. I feel eyes on me, very slowly I turn my head and he's standing right there. His eyes are scanning me, but he never looks me in the eye. Finally we make eye contact. There is lust in his eyes, they are changing from dark green to light green, going back and forth seconds apart. It's like he is struggling with something. He looks so damn sexy right now, I wish he could be in this beautiful tub with me.

"I can."

"Whoa, how did you do that?"

"Just ask me, and I'll join you. I'll make slow, sweet love to you, love."

Why do I have to love him, I'm in a strange place. This is not the room I've seen. He must have taken me to another home in Arizona, I hope. I do love him, but this right here is wrong, you don't take someone's choice away.

"I'm sorry, I can't."

"Okay, I understand. I'll wait until you are ready."

"Ready? Ready for what?"

"You are beautiful, but I'm referring to when you're done with your bath, but I see you want to know how long I'll wait for you." He comes closer, kneeling at the bath, and our faces are so close. I smell his breath, it smells delicious. "I will wait until the end of time for you, Marilyn, because you are worth waiting for, my zell." I can't say anything. No one has ever spoke like that to me. My heart is racing, my body is melting and I need to kiss him. I can't help myself. I lean forward and our lips barely touch, a moan escapes his mouth, "Mmm". The kiss deepens, and he gently coaxes me to open my mouth. His hands slide into the tub, caressing my body. I should stop him, pull away, but I can't. I want him, my kidnapper, the man who is holding me against my will- I love and want him. I'm out of my mind. Before I can push him away, Showken is in the bath with me, and he is only wearing pants, nothing else. He smells so good. Our hands and legs are entwined with each other, our lips pressed together.

"Please say yes, I need you to say yes."

He holds my face with both hands, pressing soft kisses on my cheeks, chin, and lips. I want to say yes, but this is just going to end badly. I haven't ever wanted a man like I want Showken.

"This is wrong, you have me here against my will, I-"

"Okay, okay. Soon, though, you will want me. I love you," he says, rising. He's out of the tub in no time, dropping his pants in front of me, the menace. I close my eyes quickly, before I can do something I regret. He walks out, and I hurry to wash my body, hoping my desire for him will lessen. I put on the dress Showken has laid out for me. This is not going to work for me. I don't wear dresses that often, and there is no bra or panties. He must plan on taking my body at some point, needing easy access. I'm no stranger to men taking what they want. In fact, it's normal in my life. I walk out of the bathroom, and Showken holds out his hand, waiting for me to take it. He has put on another pair of dark green pants, with no shirt or shoes. Damn, he looks hot!

"Let's take a walk."

"Well, that's nice of you, to let your captive take a walk," I say. He raises a brow at me, and I sigh, placing my hand in his.

"You are so going to owe me, beautiful." He grins as we leave his room. Holy shit, there are really long halls everywhere. The floor is beautiful, with sparkles of green leading to his door. I look at the walls all covered in jewels, I reach out and touch one. They feel real, beautiful.

"These jewels mean nothing to me, you are more precious than any jewel," Showken says, smiling. I'm in shock. Where am I? We begin to walk, passing what look like workers washing walls. I notice they bow as we pass. I think they are mumbling something, but I'm not sure. Do they speak another language? I think I remember Showken saying 'zell' to me earlier.

"What does zell mean?" I ask. He smiles hugely, giving me the pleasure of those dimples.

"Zell means beloved," he looks at me, shaking his head. "You are my beloved, come, lets find food." We continue our walk, and now I'm glad he's with me. There are some strange people around. They are looking at me weirdly. We reach a courtyard. There are people all around and I recognize some, his brothers are here. Showken's brother Layern approaches me.

"Hello Marilyn, welcome." He waves his hand for a woman to come over. She looks elegant and classy. Her hair is long and jet-black. She approaches me and her eyes are freaking mesmerizing. I can't stop looking at her.

"Love, this is my sister, Cess." His sister, he never said he had a sister.

"Hello Marilyn, I'm so excited you came. You're going to love it here," she says, enthusiastically. What does she mean 'I came'? I didn't come, I was brought here, and where is here?

"Showken kidnapped me," I snap. Maybe she could convince him to let me go.

"What? DRAKEN!!!" She yells. This fine ass man shows up, out of nowhere.

"Princess, before you say anything, Showken has good reason." His voice is so deep.

I look at Showken, who has a silly grin on his face. Does he find this funny? Crazy men.

"Cess, I had to bring her. Things got out of control, plus Hawken and Warton were being assholes."

She looks at Showken, Layern and the new guy with long, black hair like hers. She looks at me.

"Well, Marilyn, I'm sorry you were forced here, but Showken will do you no harm, neither will my husband or anyone in this land, Molla, we'll make sure, right, Draken?"

"Of course, but she's safe with Showken. He'll be good to you," he says to me.

He pats Showken on the back and starts to speak in a different language. What is he saying, but then they both smile at each other, and boy, do they look good. I notice Layern is just watching me. I don't need this creepy stuff.

"Marilyn, you think I'm weird, I'm not," Layern says, calmly. "I think if you relax some and let go of the past you will feel better, and by the way, we are all dragons, except for Cess." His eyes are very blue. He's handsome, too. I can't look at him like that, he's Showken's brother. Damn, there are too many fine men here. I need Jazz here. Regardless of how he looks, me letting go of the past is none of his business.

"Layern, I don't believe in dragons, and don't talk about my past." I glare.

"Leave her alone. Love, food sounds good, right? I'm starving," Showken says, leading me away. He turns around and mouths something, but I can't tell what it is he said. I'm more focused on the area, and how perfect it looks, too perfect. The flowers, the grass, even the pretty, colorful butterflies are amazing. We reach a table with all kinds of food and it looks perfect, too, nothing out of place.

"What would you like, precious?"

"I'm not hungry, I just would like to know something," I say. My stomach is not going to last, the food smells delicious.

"Yes, I'll answer any questions, love, if you eat first." He smiles. I roll my eyes and he laughs out loud. I can't help but smile.

"Fine, I'll eat something, give me a plate."

"No, you point to what you want, love. I usually wouldn't come over, as I never have to inform them what I want."

"Them? Who are 'them'?"

"Oh, we have servants, and to fix our own food would be an insult to them. They enjoy serving us. Now point, and we can go sit." I point to a few items. He walks me away, and we go up some stairs. I look around, noticing all of his brothers moving up the stairs, and even some men I haven't seen before. We finally sit, and Cess and Draken are sitting near us, too. They look really in love.

"Who are all these people? And I thought we were going for a walk?"

"We're going for a walk after we eat, and beautiful, this is my family; brothers, sisters, cousins, uncles, only one aunt." He smiles as they all seem to be watching us, did they hear us speaking? I'm sure we were whispering.

"Yes, we can hear very well, Marilyn, especially when we are at home. The distance is unbelievable," Layern says, nodding to the woman placing food in front of him. I notice him winking at her. She smiles back.

"Why is everyone watching us, Showken? Do they all know how you got me here?"

"No, but I'm sure they are staring because I've never had a girl eat with the family," Showken says, chuckling. What is funny?

"Showken, I-"

"You have to eat, and then we will walk. Oh, dessert you can skip, I have dessert for you, later." He leans close to my ear, whispering. I feel my body heat rising, and I just want out of this dress. I should not get this hot with him. I bet he has a box of cupcakes, too. I'm not having any part of his tricks to get me in bed.

"I'll introduce you to my family later, besides, if I come too close to Hawken or Warton, you will meet my dragon in a bad way."

"You're not a dragon, and you need to seek help."

"I am a dragon, and I will show you, if you promise not to run."

"I will run only if I can escape from you." I smile at him and he smiles back. I just enjoy our going back and forth. We eat and everyone is laughing, talking, even dancing to the music being played. We finally finish, I can't eat that much, but Showken eats four plates of food. The plates are huge, too.

"You ready for our walk?"

"Yes, I am." He stands waiting for me as I push away from the table. Everyone stops speaking and gives us curious stares, some not so pleasant. I see his mother sitting a little higher than we were, and she gives me a nod. I frown, hoping people are not condoning his bad behavior.

"Come on, beautiful, and stop frowning, you only make me want you more."

"If we are going for a walk I need shoes, Showken."

"No you don't, the ground will not harm you. I told you I'm the beast, everything else is harmless to you."

"So, you are harmful?" I ask. We walk away from the others, following a path into the woods. I'm a little scared going into the woods with Showken, but it looks too pretty to hold danger. The trees are bigger than I've ever seen before. The ground is soft on my feet, and I see fruit trees scattered throughout as we walk.

"Well Marilyn, ask away." We stop walking in front of a shiny green bench. I walk over and sit down.

"It's so hard to be angry at you when you're being so nice. What do you want from me?"

"I only want you to know the truth about me, and I want you."

"Why did you bring me here?"

"The situation was going to get out of control. I didn't want you to meet my dragon like that, so I did what I thought was best. My brothers didn't have any regard for your safety, I'm sorry."

"You're sorry? Showken, you kidnapped me. You can't keep me here."

"I won't keep you here, but I can. If you give me three days, that's all I ask, and if you still want to go after that, I will set you free."

"Showken, you think you're a dragon. We are off to a bad start. I will tell you this is a nice country, where exactly are we?" He gives me a wicked grin. I like it. I start biting on my lip.

"I'm a dragon, love, and you met him once in a dream, but I will introduce you to him now, don't run, I'll chase you." He smiles, running into the forest. I few moments later I hear a loud roar. The sound effects are awesome out here. I continue to sit and the bench starts to tremble. What in the world is going on? I stand and the ground is moving some. I hear huge footsteps coming close.

"Showken, this shit is not funny. Get your ass out here." I hear the roar again. Damn, this is a forest, maybe it's a lion, I've never heard a real lion in the woods. "I'm not playing with you, come out," I say and my voice trembles with fear. I'm nervous now; it sounds like it's really huge and scary. Shit, I'm scared. The trees start to sway, how big is this lion? A huge green head pushes through the trees. The eyes are huge. It looks at me and I can't move, it steps in front of me. Holy shit, he's a fucking dragon, or he has one as a pet, either way I'm gone. I take off in a full sprint. I'm good at track. I'm stopped in my tracks as a wing lands in front of me. This thing has wings?

"Okay, Showken, please, I can't take this. I'm scared," I say, crying. The beast lies down on the ground. It's green and scary. It moans on the ground. I cover my face, pleading with Showken to come back. I have seen a lot of shit in my life, but a fucking dragon tops everything. The creature just stays down, head to the ground, watching me.

"Showken?"

It moans. Oh, I'm freaking out. Is that a yes?

"Showken, if this is you, blink twice," I say, sniffling.

It blinks twice. I look into its eyes and they seem familiar. Oh, maybe- wait, he's a dragon? I take a seat on the ground. We both just stare at each other. I wonder if I can touch him? Do I even want to? I rise from the ground, and the thing stays still. I move closer.

"Showken, can I touch you?"

He moans again, but almost a happy sound, if a dragon can have one. I walk closer, until I'm right in front of it.

"Please don't move, or I'm gonna shit in my pants."

It blinks and its eyes are really green. I reach out and touch the snout. It's soft; most stories say dragon skin is rough. I get a boost of brave, and move to the side. I rub the snout, causing a soft sound to come out, and the beast's skin becomes very soft and starts turning different shades of green.

"Showken, I need you human, please. We have to talk," I say, backing away. The creature rises and walks into the woods. I watch as it disappears and then I start crying again. Why did this have to happen to me? I'm captured for life; he's a beast, or dragon as he says. Showken comes from the forest with a wrap around his waist. He's a dragon-shifter. I love a dragon.

SHOWKEN

She's handling it better than I thought, but I can sense her fear. She cries as if she thinks I would harm her, I would never do that. I'm glad she touched me. My beast loves her, and I want her so badly.

"You ran," I say, coming to a stop a few feet in front of her.

"You're a dragon, with big teeth," she says, looking at me. I wonder . . .

"I scared you?"

"Yes!"

"I'm sorry for that, too; I keep saying sorry to you, I'm not used to that," I say, softly. I take a step toward her, and she stands still. I don't want her frightened of me.

"Do you eat, umm, people?" I tilt my head a little, annoyed that she would think that.

"You've seen what I eat, and anything I eat on you, love, you like," I say, stressing the words. "I know you have been given more information than you would want," I sigh. "But give me three days for me to show you how much I love you, please. If you don't want me to touch you I won't, if you want me to sleep on the floor I will. I just want you to give me a chance. I had to show you everything first before we could move forward."

"Can you take me back to your room? I need to lie down." She looks confused.

"Yes, baby, I'll take you right now." I walk over, and without giving her a chance to tense up, I transport us immediately to my room. She steps back, looking at me strangely. I want to kiss her body so badly. She climbs into bed.

"Three days, Showken, and then if I want to leave, you take me home."

"Okay, I will, I promise, but I hope you stay." I grin. I feel really good about having these next three days to seduce her into staying with me forever. I need her.

"Showken, where are we?"

"Cortamagen, love."

"Not Earth?"

"No, Kalin is our planet."

"Okay," she says, and drifts off to sleep. I'm not sure if this is some defense system she's in, but she's too calm right now. I need to talk with one of my brothers. I will stay here for a while and just watch her sleep. I can't touch her, but I can sit and hope she stays.

***

It's morning, and she's still asleep. She hasn't moved the entire night, I hope she's okay. I watch her sleep, wondering if she still loves me. I told Layern to meet me outside my bedroom in a few minutes. I sniff the air, and I smile, knowing my brother is out there in the hall waiting. I walk out the door, and he's leaning against the wall.

"Hello, brother."

"Hello, you slept on the floor, very nice of you."

"Well, believe me, it took all my strength not to climb into bed with her."

"Yes, I know," Layern says. "Listen, I know why you asked me to come and speak with you. She does love you, but I told you she's guarded, too. There are some things she's hiding in her heart. Marilyn is in shock about the dragon, also. Plus, she's not sure about you and her. The only thing I will tell you is, in three days, if you haven't convinced her, she'll leave."

"You know, you were supposed to make me feel better," I say.

"Well, you can always go to our mother and get more details," Layern smiles. I roll my eyes, knowing she would be more accurate, but I'm in this mess because she decided to send Warton, and her errand boy Hawken told me I was running out of time. I took Marilyn from Earth against her will. I won't lose her.

"Thanks, brother. I've been meaning to ask you, how are the ladies treating you?"

He gives the famous Draglen smile. "Oh, brother, I'm making up for lost time. I thought I would never get over Malio, but I'm moving on with my life."

"I'm glad she's not with you, and that she decided to be with our cousin, Joflor."

"She did, but now I'm over her, and the ladies are reaping the benefit of my pent-up sexual frustration." We smile at each other. I hear Marilyn moving around in the room.

"Well, have fun, brother. I'm on a deadline, and need to get started right away, proving my love for her."

"Good luck, I hope you get the girl. Wow, never thought you, of all the brothers, could love any female."

"Neither did I," I say, glancing at my door. She's out of bed. "Talk later, brother, my future Wella is awake." I smile, opening my door to find Marilyn eating the food I had waiting for her. She glances at me, and continues to eat. Shit, I wanted to ask Layern more about her thoughts.

"Good morning, love, well actually it's afternoon, but morning somewhere, right?" I joke.

"I miss Bruiser." Oh, I should have told her he's here. Bruiser loves running and playing around the grounds.

"Wait, one second. I'll call him to come."

"He's here?"

"Yes, he's here, I went back for him. I know how much he means to you. He's just been running around the grounds. He loves it here." Her eyes are watery. I walk over to the door, and growl loudly. This is a call, especially made for certain animals, and dogs are on the list. In a matter of minutes I can smell him coming. He's running at full speed, too. Soon, he rushes into the room and goes straight to Marilyn. She breaks down when she sees him, crying and hugging him. I watch, as she seems so happy to see him. I only want her happy. I hope she gives me a chance.

"Thank you, Showken, thank you so much," she says, looking up at me. If she asked for the stars I would try to get her one. I love this woman.

"You're welcome, love. Now that we are all united again, I thought you might like to see what I do when I'm in the castle."

"So dragons live in castles, that's true?"

"We live in castles, as I'm a prince in my land, and if you stay you will become my princess, come, we can talk about this later. I have more clothes stocked for you and this time there are a couple of pairs of jeans, only a couple, because we dragons love to see our women in dresses."

"Really? I'm wearing jeans today." She walks over to the closet area. She looks for a few seconds and turns around to me.

"You had them buy a store? Showken, this is way too much, I can never wear all of these clothes."

"Yes you can, besides, sometimes dresses can tear," I say, smiling. I miss her body so much, but I'll wait.

"I'll get dressed," she smiles. Marilyn is in a better mood now that she has Bruiser around. After she had seen my dragon, she shut down. I hope she will grow to love my dragon as much as he loves her. I sit on the bed, enjoying a perfect view of her body. She takes off the dress from yesterday and is bare. Her body is perfect.

"Showken, where are some panties? And I need a bra."

"No panties, and especially not a bra. First, it can get really hot. Second, you're going to wish you wore a dress. I only have on pants myself. Underclothes are an Earth thing."

"I'm from Earth, and wearing jeans without panties is nasty."

"I like nasty, and you are in my land now, love. Put on the green shirt," I say, winking at her. She blushes, yes. She wants me; I can win her.

"The only things not green are the jeans, Showken. A green shirt, I'm pretty sure, is what I will be wearing."

"Yes, I hope you like green."

"It's okay. Do you have green everything because, umm, your dragon is green?"

"That is part of the reason, but my dragon is green because I can get jealous, and my beast can get angry when it happens."

"The color matches the personality?"

"Exactly, come, love. I can't stay in a room like this when you are looking amazing in those jeans and that shirt is hugging your breasts and waist like that."

She smiles again, and I hold my hand out for her. I want her to see one of my hobbies. As we walk to my private room, she asks a lot of questions. I answer them all. Her questions are not too bad. We finally make it to my room and I open the door, escorting her in.

"Oh, wow, this is amazing. Have you done everything in here?"

"Yes, I love art. Using my hands is what I like to do. I can give you a demonstration if you like?"

"Umm, no, I don't think so."

"Your mind and body want me, precious, but I was talking about painting something for you." I smile. She is gathering information, debating within herself about me. I know this. If she releases everything to me, I will give her happy days forever.

"You want to paint right now?"

"It would be my pleasure," I say, walking to a cabinet with my supplies. I pull out what I need, and start placing it next to a table. I pick up a bench, setting it in front of the window where you can see the sky. Yes this is perfect.

"You are pretty serious about art?"

"Yes, love, I am. Now, I need you and Bruiser to have a seat on the bench. It will only take five minutes. I am faster than the artists you have heard of," I wink. Bruiser is at the bench ready for his painting. She reluctantly goes over a take a seat. It's perfect; I draw her and Bruiser, with the sky in the background. I begin to draw, the convincing of Marilyn has started. It's not very long before I've finished. I turn the picture around, and it's her and Bruiser on the bench, smiling, and me in the background, flying in the air, protecting her.

"Oh wow, this is a beautiful picture. The details of me on the picture are amazing, and Bruiser looks so handsome. Thanks, Showken."

"You are welcome, but now I want you to come and paint anything you want." I chuckle, because her expression goes from pleasant to horrified, but I know she can do this.

"I don't paint, Showken. I'm not doing it."

"Yes you are, nobody is allowed in here, but you and our pet are always welcome," I say, stalking her, she holds her hands up, saying no. I'm not listening to her. I want her to experience painting at least once. She tries to make a dash for the door, but I'm much faster. I chuckle at her attempt. I pick her up and carry her to the paint. She laughs, and Bruiser barks his agreement.

"Don't run from me, love," I say, setting her on her feet. "Now, pick a brush and any color, I will work on this piece with you." She sighs, but chooses a small brush. I pick green and she tries to pick red.

"Baby, red is not allowed on the board."

"Why?"

"Domlen loves that color, and you're my girl, not his."

"Okay, pink it is."

"Wow, pink and green are perfect together, what are we painting?"

"You're the artist, Picasso, you choose."

"Brush anywhere you like, and I'll follow," I say. Standing

behind her, I move closer so that my body is touching her. She gasps, feeling my erection. I wrap one arm around her waist. "Painting is all about emotion, zell."

"Okay, I'll try." She turns her head, and before she can say no, I steal a kiss from her sweet lips. As her hand moves, my brush follows hers, creating patterns. Every now and then I lean in to smell her hair better. With my brush I start mixing our colors. My hand starts moving in slow, deliberate circles on the top of her pelvic bone. I feel the heat rising between both of us. Bruiser barks, he wants to go out of the room. I open the door using mind control, and let him out.

"Showken, what are you doing?"

"Loving you," I say, spinning her around. I take my brush and move slowly up and down her cheeks. "See, baby, with painting you have to be gentle. It's like making love." Her heart rate increases, and I send her heat through my touch. Quickly I push my hand inside her jeans, finding her soaking. Yes, I want you, too. "Ohh," she whispers. I find her clitoris and start a fast rub, as she drops her brush her hands are on my bare chest, leaving pink everywhere. Leaning down, I place a soft kiss on her lips, and she opens for me. I can't stop myself; we are on the bench with her on top. I hold her tight, not giving her a chance to change her mind. I rip that shirt off her back. We are kissing roughly, hands and paint are everywhere. I still have my brush. I flip her over so she's on her back, and removing the shredded shirt, I take my brush and write 'Showken' on her body, painting her green everywhere.

"Mine," I say, sliding my pants down my body.

"Hurry." Yes, her body needs me like I need her. She's not leaving me ever. I slide inside and she fits around me like a glove. I have to savor this; slowing, I begin thrusting in and out of her.

"Ahh, mmm," she moans. Her breath is racing.

"Whose is it?" I ask softly in her ear. She tries to speak, but I thrust hard into her, causing the bench to slide forward. "Love, whose is it?"

"Yours." I slam again.

"Name, say it."

"SHOWKEN!! It's yours, baby, yours."

"How long?" I slow the pace, giving her a break. I'm so in love with her, my body hurts.

"Huh, ahh," I slam harder. She screams out. "FOREVER!"

"Yes, zell, forever you are mine," I say, beginning to kiss her neck, as I continue to give her orgasm after orgasm. "I love you so much, beautiful, so much." We continue our lovemaking for a few more hours, until she begs me for a break. I hold her until she falls asleep. I vanish us into my room, tucking her into bed.

I make myself a drink and I smell Hawken. I hurry to the door, closing it gently behind me.

"What the fuck do you want?" I glare.

"Fuck you, Showken. You don't scare me one bit, our mother says get your ass to the garden."

"I'm not going anywhere, Marilyn will not leave my sight!" I snap.

"I'm here to guard your precious-" Before he says another word, I'm shooting fire at him. I hit him squarely in the chest and he goes down. I walk over to him.

"Get your ass to the door, to guard Marilyn, if you move I'm going to really fuck you up. I told you I'm not Draken," I say, making a run for the garden. I could have vanished there, but after sex sometimes you can get weak, I never want to be unprepared. I get to the garden to find my mother waiting for me. Shit, she must be angry. She doesn't speak, so I guess addressing her the traditional way is what she's waiting for, fuck I'm in trouble.

"Queen Nala, Mother of Draglen descendants, you summoned me," I say. She glares at me.

"Showken, if you burn your brother one more time, I will issue you a punishment, are we clear?"

"Yes, Queen," I say through clenched teeth. Shit, he always has something smart to say.

"I thought we were clear?"

"We are clear, Queen."

"Why would you tell the human she could go back in three days? That's not going to happen, my son."

"I- permission to speak freely, Queen."

"Permission granted."

"It's my decision, and if she chooses to leave I will let her."

"If you want this to be granted, my son, you must be willing to wipe her memories of you, and that includes her pesty little friend. She can't know you either." Damn it, I don't want to wipe her memories, she could change her mind and want me later. If I wipe them, then it's done forever. I can't be with her then.

"I'm happy you understand the seriousness of this issue. It's not up for discussion, or any negotiations.

"I understand," I snap.

"Are you angry?" she glares.

"No, Mother, I'm sorry. I will make sure that if she chooses to go I will erase her memory."

"Thank you, my son, now you can continue to play with her."

"Do you know?"

"Are you asking me to tell you if she's going to stay? I will not answer that, because it will depend on you," she says, turning and vanishing into thin air. I run back to my room, where my hurting brother is glaring and spitting fire at my walls.

"You had better get those wounds looked at," I say, pushing him aside to enter my room. I hurry back into bed with Marilyn, pulling her close. She's still asleep. Please stay, I whisper.

MARILYN

I open my eyes to see green eyes staring at me. Then I remember Showken and me with the paint. I did not plan for that to happen. It seems like I can't resist this man, or dragon- I'm not sure what to call him.

"Hello, beautiful."

"Hello, what time is it?"

"It's nightfall, I wanted to take you flying with me," he says, removing a string of hair from my face.

"Flying? Showken, what do you mean?" I start biting my lip. I'm nervous about his dragon; it looks scary.

"If you don't want to that's fine, I thought you might want to ride my dragon."

"That sounds nasty," I say. We both laugh, because it does sound a little kinky.

"Well, what about just taking a bath and talking," he suggests. I like that idea better. I don't have the heart to tell Showken his dragon is like a nightmare come true. How can I think about staying, when all I see is a scary dragon?

"I think I would prefer that," I say softly. I've never been shy, but being around Showken makes me shy, almost at a loss for words. I'm in awe at how he is, so generous, kind, loving, and the best lover a girl could ever want. The problem is he's a dragon. I can't forget that.

"I'll start the water, wait for me, or you will be on the floor, love." He smiles. That smile gets me every time. When I saw that dragon, I couldn't believe it. Who would have thought, other than Earth, that planets like this existed? I mean, we hear about it in movies and tabloids, but I'm starting to think aliens are on Earth. If we have dragons, then anything is possible. Showken comes naked from the bathroom. My mouth goes dry. He is so free with his body. He walks over to the bed and slowly pulls the covers down my body. How does he make me hot just by doing this? I see pink and green paint on my body. Then I notice the paint on him. I guess he doesn't care.

"You ready, zell?"

"Yes, I'm ready." He bends down and lifts me off the bed, carrying me to the tub. He steps in, still holding me until we are in the water. My body feels like jelly. He pulls me into his chest.

"Say yes you'll stay, zell."

"I thought three days was the agreement."

"It's still the agreement, I thought you could decide early," he smiles. "Early is always good, right?" I find myself blushing. I never blush, but Showken the human makes me blush. Showken the huge dragon makes me want to run.

"Can we just enjoy the bath and talk?"

"Yes, I want to talk. Tell me, love, where did you go when you left the bar?" he asks. Fuck, I'm not trying to make him disgusted with me. I can't tell him that. "Love, why are you thinking so hard about that question?"

"No reason, I went to a old friend and cried."

"I'm so sorry about that, baby. In my defense, you were giving me the cold shoulder and I wanted you to know I'm worth it."

"You are, but that was pretty fucked up, Showken, and you know it."

"I know, that will never happen again because you, zell, are my everything," he says, stalking me in the tub. I move backwards until I finally hit the end. He raises a brow. "Are you running from me?"

"I'm not running, just didn't want our conversation to end," I smile. "You say you're a prince, right?"

"That's right."

"Well, will you be a king one day?"

"No. My brother Draken is heir to the throne. I will always be

184

royalty, though."

"Are you okay with that?"

"More than okay. Draken struggles with this huge responsibility, but he has Cess now, and she will make sure he does fine."

"How many brothers do you have?"

"I have eight brothers and one sister, there are ten of us all together. My turn. Could you leave Jasmine and her child for love?" he asks. My mind drifts to Jazz and all of our good times. My only human friend besides Bruiser. I'm not sure. She has been my rock for so long. She's not just a friend; she's my family, the only family I have, and I'm all she has. Showken has a huge family, but if I leave, it's like I abandon her.

"I take it from your silence you don't know if you could," he says, sadly. This is the hardest decision ever in my life. I can't leave her; she might not make it.

"Jazz is my only family, her and Rachel, my goddaughter. If I leave, I take the only family she has away," I sigh. "I'm not sure, Showken."

"I see. How do you like my land so far?"

"Well I haven't seen that much, but it's very pretty," I say softly. I don't want to hurt him.

"After we bathe I can take you around more, there's so much to do here," he says, sweetly.

"Where would you take me?"

"I would take you dancing first." He wriggles in the water. I remember him dancing, him and his brothers at the bar. I can't dance- not one bit. I have two left feet when it comes to dancing.

"Dancing, nope, pick another place."

"Dancing scares you, well you happen to be with one of the best dancers in the family, so dancing it shall be," he says. "Besides, dancing is something we do here a lot." He takes the oil, dropping some into the water, and pouring some into his hands.

"Massage?" he asks. This dragon man is too good to be true.

"Yes, I would love one."

"Stay facing me." I blink. I'm feeling shy again. His hands come to my shoulders, rubbing me, and it feels so good. His eyes are piercing through mine. I feel his hands move to my breasts, squeezing softly, and hard, going back and forth. I want to take my eyes off him, but I can't, he has me captivated. I moan out load when he pinches my nipples. They instantly harden. His eyes never leave mine. His hands are so hot, literally. It feels like the best heating pad ever. His hands slip lower, and he starts rubbing my hips hard. My lips fall open. I want his hands on me. My body is jumping inside.

"Showken?"

"Yes, zell," he smiles. I can't help my breathing; it's going crazy.

"Can you touch me?" I beg.

"Of course, love, patience." He takes one hand and cups my sex, while continuing to squeeze my hips. This feels so good. I throw my head back, enjoying his touch. I'm about to orgasm when I feel him pulling me on top of him. My body fits him perfectly. I slid his sex inside of me, and my body goes crazy. I can't hold my screams "OHHHHH!!"

"Yes, love, I'm yours, take me," he whispers in my ear. He wraps his arms around me and we get a rhythm going. Up, down, back and forth. Every time I'm with him it makes me want to stay. We make love in the tub, and once in the closet, before we are dressed to go dancing. I mean dressed as much as possible. I notice all of the men only wear pants, and the women wear dresses with no shoes.

After a long walk, we make it to the park. My feet are hurting, but Showken kneels down, wrapping his hands around my ankle, and the sore feeling goes away.

"If you decide to stay, pain in your feet from walking won't happen, you will be a part of me." he says.

"Would I become a dragon?"

"No, you must be born a dragon, love, but you will have protection, I promise."

He smiles, pulling me over to what looks like a party. The guests are so excited to see Showken, bowing and applauding as he walks into an area where people are dancing. I try to pull away, but his grip tightens. He is a very strong man, dragon man.

"Showken, I don't want to embarrass you, please, I'll watch you. There are plenty of women around who will dance. I won't get jealous," I plead. The music stops. Shit. All eyes are on us. I don't want to do this. Then Showken speaks.

"My people, my zell does not dance often, so I will teach her, but if I get a glimpse of anyone finding amusement in this I will be disappointed, which will come with punishment." The people begin to speak out.

"Prince Showken, we would never do such a dishonorable thing" one man says. Others speak.

"Prince Showken, never would we do such a horrible thing."

"Thank you, my people, resume the music, and dance, everyone, dance," he says, smiling. He makes our fingers slide together, and starts swaying his hips at me. Oh my, dirty freaky dancing. I thought he danced good at the bar, but he is really dancing now. I'm just moving side to side. I don't know how to move like everyone else. People are giving me encouraging nods. I blush, not knowing what to do.

"Love, I'm going to take the lead," he says and I feel like Baby from Dirty Dancing when she was learning to dance. I'm not going to learn after one night. We dance about three more songs before going to eat with his people. Showken is so down to earth; he listens to their problems, and even vows to help some of them. He doesn't act like a prince at all. He takes me to a lake where he tries to convince me to skinny dip with him. He says mermaids are in the water, but they won't bother me. The night is fun, I know the time is ticking and soon I will have to make a decision. I'm not looking forward to that. We are back at the castle in no time.

"You said you have a sister, why haven't you introduced me to her, or the rest of your brothers?"

He pauses for a moment and looks me in the eye.

"You only get to meet them if you are going to stay, I'm not allowed to introduce you to family unless they come to you, because until you decide if you will stay, you are a threat."

"A threat, how the hell am I a threat?"

"You know our secret and can expose us."

"You could kill me, why would I do that? Besides, no one would believe me. I can't believe them." I'm pissed. I'm not good enough even to meet. That doesn't help with me wanting to stay.

"I know you're upset, but you must look at it from their point of view; if you change your mind, you will want to tell someone about this place. It would make business hard for us if people think we are dragons, because we do disappear sometimes for months. Humans just think we own an island or something."

"Showken, stop making fucking excuses, there's no reason that they should be rude to me like that. In fact, I notice none of your brothers, the ones I do know, come up to me except Layern." I am tapping my feet. I'm pissed. I call for Bruiser, but he doesn't come. Showken growls, and I hear barking. Even my own dog answers to them. I start walking, not even knowing where I am going.

"Love, where are you going? Our room is the other way," he says, keeping up with my pace.

"I'm not sure, maybe if I run into somebody, they can pretend I don't exist!" I snap. "Plus that Cess girl is human."

"That's my brother's Wella, she lives here, and this is her land now. You are not sure if you want to stay," he snaps. Oh, so he's not so perfect after all, taking up for this wrong.

"Showken, you will not sleep in the bed with me tonight. Maybe, maybe three days is too long- I can decide now you know," I say. He's in my face fast. His eyes are full of anger.

"You promised three days, don't go back on your word to me," he growls. Oh shit, I made him mad. I'm mad too, but his mad is scarier than my mad. Nothing is said for like five seconds. He swings me around and starts walking me the other way. We pass Domlen, and he just winks at me. I give him the finger, and his mouth falls open. Yes, these fuckers think they're better. We finally make it to the room. Showken slams the door right in front of Bruiser's face, who I've been waiting for, been calling him and he never came.

"WHY DID YOU DO THAT? LET HIM IN NOW!" I yell.

"NO!" He is pacing back and forth in front of the door. I can tell he is pissed. After a couple of minutes, he stops pacing.

"You can't hurt me like that, zell." He looks at me. I'm seated on the bed and just watching, hoping he doesn't turn into that dragon.

"It hurts me that I'm not good enough to be introduced."

"You are good enough, don't you understand? I'm asking you to stay with me forever, to be my Wella, my wife, everything. If you say no, I have to keep going as if nothing ever happened. You are hurting me," he says, frustrated. My hands are over my face and I'm crying now. I should have just told him to let me go, agreeing to three days is only prolonging what we both know is going to happen, I'm going home. I don't want to leave my home.

"Showken, in the morning, please take me and Bruiser home," I say. I look up to find him standing there looking at me in shock.

SHOWKEN

My heart is breaking. She wants to go home. I shouldn't have yelled. This is my fault. How can I let her go? I love her. If she leaves, she'll take a piece of my heart with her.

"You really want to go home?"

"Yes," she says. The tears flowing down her face say she's torn. How can I fix this? I want her to stay.

"Please reconsider, I'm sorry for yelling, and Bruiser, I didn't mean to do that. I just got angry. It won't happen again," I say, taking a step forward.

"Please, Showken, don't come closer, this is so hard, but I have to go, I don't belong here."

"Yes you do, you belong with me." I can't think straight; my beast is tugging at me. I need to fly. I can't stay in here right now. "I need to take a walk or something, I'll be back," I say, walking out of the room. I race to the field and change into my dragon in no time. The night air is refreshing. My beast needs this right now; the thought of losing Marilyn is unbearable. I'm flying when I feel someone behind me. I turn and my beast blows fire, I see it's Draken and he dodges the fireball, but shoots one back. He flies ahead, landing on a cliff. I follow him, even though I don't feel like talking. He shifts into human form and I do the same. There are wraps waiting on a rock for us.

"Showken, everyone heard you and Marilyn, why did you tell her that?" he snaps. I don't have time for the great Draken today.

"She fucking asked, okay, I didn't think it would turn out like this, now she wants to go home tomorrow."

"We heard it all, plus you fucking yelled at her, do you know you shook the castle? Princess is very upset with you right now. You need to think fast, brother, because our father wants her gone tonight."

"She's not leaving tonight, in the morning or ever."

"Showken, you have lost it, if she wants to go she will, even if I take her, and I will erase her memory." This asshole is only thinking about himself, if this were Cess he would think differently.

"I haven't lost anything, including Marilyn," I growl. "And if Father wants her gone, then I will leave this land and join another part of Kalin."

"Listen to yourself, you can't keep her if she wants to go. Showken. I will hold Father off until morning, so think of something fast," Draken growls. He turns back into his beast and flies back.

How am I going to fix this? She's hurt and angry. I turn back into my beast and head home. I find Marilyn in bed. She's not asleep.

"Love, please can we talk?"

"Nothing to talk about, Showken, I just hope I can get my jobs back when I get home." She sniffs.

"Please, don't cry, I'm so sorry, please, please, I'm begging you, don't leave me."

"I'm sorry, this is not going to work."

"Why?"

"Can I have the room to myself, please?" she asks. I feel a tear drop down my cheek.

"Yes, you can." I turn and walk out the door. I lean against the wall, letting the tears run down my face. She will not even know who I am if I let her go. The night goes by slowly, giving me time to start grieving my zell.

***

The next morning the door opens, and she has on a pair of jeans and a green t-shirt. Her eyes are puffy from crying all night. I could hear her. Bruiser is waiting beside me.

"Please, love, don't go."

"I have to, you shouldn't ever have brought me here in the first place, and you could have taken me home." My insides are crumbling.

"How do I get home? The faster the better," she says, avoiding my eyes.

"We can go to the garden," I say, holding out my hand. She takes my hand, and we walk to the garden. I stop just before we walk outside.

"You don't love me?"

"I do love you, I love you so much it hurts me, it's killing me, but I have to go. You will find someone who is better than me, Showken, this is not for me, I am nothing."

"You think you're not good enough for me? You are more than good; you are the best. I will never love again if you leave me. I won't."

"Then you won't love, because I'm leaving." We walk through the entrance and all my brothers are there. My mother and father are both waiting also. I feel like I'm dying. I walk her to the center of the garden, a space where we transport back and forth. Bruiser is at my feet shaking, he doesn't want to leave. What is her issue?

"You don't love me?" I ask, looking at her.

"I don't want to do this with you," She sighs. "I told you to leave me alone. I'm not good for you, heck, I'm no good for anyone. You should have taken my advice, had you a couple of beers with your brothers, but nooo, you had to pursue me." She holds her head down, but I hear the tremble in her voice. I place my hand under her chin to lift her head. The tears are coming down like a river. I don't want to hurt her, she can't see that. I will let her go, but I will never love again.

"I don't want you to cry, love. I want you to stay with me, love me, and I love you. Why is that such a hard thing for you to accept?" I say, wiping tears away. She shakes her head. I don't know what I can do? I'm in turmoil. How can I take her back to earth and erase her memory? I'm not that strong. I glance at Layern, knowing he will be able to do this. The garden is silent, every creature has gone quiet. Layern walks towards us. I see the look of confusion on her face. He and I exchange a nod. Marilyn looks at me with those beautiful grey eyes, I lean down and press a soft kiss on her lips.

"Showken, I-"

"I love you always." I say, turning and exiting the garden. I can't watch her leave, I won't. I vanish into my room. Pacing back and forth in my room, I think of how I should never have brought her here. I'm the fool for falling in love with her. My anger is overpowering me, my entire thought process is my beast right now. After destroying my bed, I go to a place in our forest and change into dragon. This is what I shall be, never going back to Earth or transforming into human form again.

MARILYN

Seeing him walk away in sorrow is so painful. I look at Layern who is holding his hand out for me. After placing my hand in his, I notice the family all leaving now. Bruiser barks at me a few times, and I do believe he's not happy about leaving either. Layern opens some kind of hole, looks like a portal. He picks up Bruiser and I rub his head, I think to myself how it's just him and me again. I hear a loud roar, and I know it's Showken. In time he will forget me, but I'll never forget him. I close my eyes, and Layern pulls me close as he walks into this very colorful portal. I'm going home.

In no time we are back at my apartment. Bruiser goes to check out the bedroom. I look around, taking a deep breath.

"Everything is fine with your jobs and your friend Jasmine, they thought you were on a vacation with Showken. You can tell your friend it didn't work out," Layern says, emotionlessly.

"Thanks."

"It's my duty to erase your memory of all you know about us, even Showken."

"Oh please don't do that, I would never say anything," I plead.

"I know you wouldn't," he says. "That's why I decided not to, not because of you, but because of my brother. He will be in misery much longer than your life span, it's only fair that you suffer too."

I'm speechless. Layern's right though, but he just doesn't know my past.

"Ok, thanks for that, I think."

"Tell me about your past, I need to understand why you would hurt my brother like that." His stare is cold. Layern is usually such a nice guy. "Yes, I am a nice guy, but my family brings out another side, the brother who is normally happy has decided to live in dragon form, because of you. I need to know why, Marilyn, right now, and about your past." He growls. Shit, I've really pissed him off.

"Well, I've never had a good life." I take a deep breath. "My mother, or the lady who birthed me into the world, only loved me for a minute. Her and my father was together a few years after I was born. I was a mistake. They both are addicts; they should have aborted me or gave me up for adoption." I shake my head walking to the kitchen. I turn on the water filling Bruiser's bowl up, and pouring food into his other bowl. Layern is watching me; his eyes going from dark blue to sky blue are really freaky.

"Continue," he says.

"After they split, my father let my mother keep me; she went through a ton of boyfriends. She never cared for me like she should. She got with this one guy named Lester. He started around age seven, touching me." Layern is listening closely. "The touching turned into him asking me to perform oral sex on him. I hated every day I opened my eyes. He became abusive and the authorities got involved when I went to school with a black eye." I find that I don't want to talk about this. I'm pacing the floor remembering my past.

"Marilyn, you need to continue, it will help."

"When I went to live with my father, I thought things would be different." I roll my eyes. "I was so stupid. Good times lasted only a few years before his lifestyle became mine. He was feeding me drugs and selling me to his dope dealer to pay off his debts, and the dope dealer was selling me too. This lasted until I was 16 years old and got the court to release me into my own care. I didn't know anything about taking care of myself. I was living on the street when I met a lady named Carmel." He raises his eyebrows at me. "I know, but even to this day I don't know her real name. She told me that she knew how I could make some money, without living on the streets. I got hooked up with a pimp and worked as a whore for about four years and used drugs until about four years ago.

When I finally got free of that life I knew that my life would never be acceptable to any man." I start crying. "Showken loving some whore like me is wrong, he deserves better. I would shame him. The only reason I'm telling you is because you will understand my decision." I say. The tears are stilling flowing down my face.

Layern walks to the kitchen, opens the fridge and pulls out a beer. He walks over and hands it to me. I open it and take a long drink, moving to the sofa.

"Now listen, Marilyn, you are so brave and strong. Thank you for sharing that with me, I think you should have told Showken," he says, calmly. "We are not a judging family. What happened to you is horrible, and in my land justice would be served far better than Earth could ever produce. You really need to rethink your decision. You still have a choice; don't let your past determine your future. My brother loves you, and we would love you in the family. I'm going to leave now, but you are not a whore, you are a survivor." He opens a portal to leave. He gives me a smile and jumps through the hole. What a life I have. I see Bruiser eating, and it makes me smile, then cry. I'm never going to love like I love him. I cry myself to sleep, right there on the sofa.

***

The next morning, my body feels like a train has hit it. Bruiser is asleep on the floor next to me, snoring. I stagger to the bathroom. After washing my face and brushing my teeth, I go to bed. Just as

I'm about to go back to sleep I hear my cell phone ringing. It says, 7:00 a.m. I really hope this is not my job, I need to sleep. But it's just Jazz.

"Wake up, I want to know how was the vacation with Showken, I mean you traveled with this hot man, give me details?"

"Jazz, really? When do I go back to work?"

"Tomorrow, but I can't wait until then, what's up, are you guys in a relationship?"

"No, in fact we are not going to see each other again." I sigh. Jasmine is really dramatic at times.

"What the fuck? Bitch, this is once in a lifetime, what did he do that is so terrible?"

"Nothing, I broke it off,"

"Ohh, no you didn't. Only a real good friend would tell you this," She pauses. "You going to get over whatever is holding you back from this man, and you going to jump right back in with him."

"No I'm not, Jazz, and if you are my friend you respect my decision," I yell. There is a long pause on the phone. She finally speaks.

"Fine."

"Fine."

"You want to see me and your god-daughter today?" I do miss them, but I need time to grieve.

"How about tomorrow, me and Bruiser will come over after work and spend the night at your place, good?"

"I guess, being you have scared off that fine man. Is all his brothers gone?"

"I'm not sure, but it will be fine," I say, trying to convince myself. How can I stop loving someone? I guess out of sight out of mind.

"Shit, Mari, I'm sorry about it, I just knew this vacation my girl would put it on him and he would be asking you to move in or something."

"Well, I don't want to talk about him," I say. I hear Bruiser barking, meaning he needs to go outside.

"I have to go, Bruiser needs to go out."

"Alright, talk later?"

"Yeah, sounds good," I say, as we both hang up the phone. I slip on some shorts with my bra and t-shirt, and slide into my sandals. I walk to the door, pick up the leash, and we both head outside, taking a walk around the complex. I finally reach the park on the other side of the apartments. Bruiser relieves himself, and we walk around some more. It's already warm, and I turn Bruiser back to our apartment. He barks a couple of times, like he sees something, but I don't see anything. I squint my eyes, and I swear, I see Showken standing in the distance, shit. I blink a couple of times, and he's not there. I quickly go back to the apartment, and once I'm in, I lock the doors. I'm not sure what I'm thinking, he's a damn dragon, if he wants in, he's damn well coming in. I walk to the kitchen and make sure Bruiser's bowls are filled with food and water. I sit on my sofa and think, could I really just have seen him?

I'm going back to sleep, I'm tired. I go back to the bed and climb in. I close my eyes, trying to sleep, but I keep seeing his green eyes staring at me, fuck.

"Showken," I whisper. There is nothing, just silence. I'm losing my mind. I start to drift off, and then I hear his voice.

"Hello, beautiful, I miss you already." I'm afraid to open my eyes. I crack open one eye and the room is empty.

"Showken, are you here?"

"Yes."

"I don't like looking like I'm talking to myself."

"Well, come home, love, I can't live without you."

"NO" I yell. I start crying again.

"Please love, don't cry. I will come back and get you if you want, just say yes."

"I can't, Showken, please, you said you would let me go."

"Beautiful, I'm a dragon prince, and a very emotional creature right now. I lied. I want you back, and have decided that I'm not going to give you up."

"What? You're going to kidnap me again?"

"No, zell. You will ask to come back, because I feel your love for me. Layern told me about your past, and I don't care about any of it, I want you home in our bed."

"Huh, no, this is not happening, you said you were going to let me go, besides I live here on Earth, where I belong."

"You belong with me, beautiful, and I'm never letting you go." I cover my face with a pillow, hoping to drown out his sexy voice.

"You are so annoying," I say.

"Beautiful, that's what attracted you to me in the beginning,"

"No, it was those amazing green eyes and that drop dead gorgeous smile that got me in trouble"

"I miss you so badly, come home, I'm not going anywhere."

"Really? I'm going to ignore you."

"Ok."

"Ok," I say. I finally find sleep and have a very peaceful rest.

***

I really needed that sleep. I stretch, glancing at the clock; it's after 1:00 in the afternoon. How could I sleep so long? I call out for Bruiser and he doesn't come, where the heck is he?

"Bruiser," I yell again. Immediately I remember my weird conversation with Showken, even though I couldn't see him. I climb out of my bed, open the nightstand and get my gun out. There better not be anything wrong with Bruiser. I tiptoe down my short hall, listening for him. Silence. Shit. I come around the corner, praying that Bruiser is ok, and there he sits next to Showken on the floor, resting his head in his lap. I stare at them both in disbelief.

"What are you doing with my dog, Showken?" I ask, staring at Bruiser, making sure he's ok.

"You were sleeping, so I decided to take Bruiser for a run in

Cortamagen," he says, calmly. My eyes are about to pop out of my head. He left the planet with my dog!

"You kidnapped my dog?" I snap.

"Beautiful, Bruiser wanted to go, he's fine, a little tired from trying to chase me, but he's relaxed." He smiles. I see them damn dimples, they're my weakness. I shuffle from side to side, nervous to see him here. The last time I saw him, he looked so sad, now he looks determined.

"Umm, Showken, what are you doing here?"

"I'm here to convince you to come home."

"I'm home, Showken," I say, low. He is staring intensely at me. My body is reacting to him. I try to look away, but I can't. I love this man; he is making this so hard. He rises from the floor, and my apartment just got real small. I feel my breathing getting faster. Wiping my forehead to make sure I'm not sweating, I take a step back.

"Love, home is with me, not here. I made a mistake by kidnapping you, as you say, but it's only because I was protecting you," he says, moving closer. I close my eyes, trying not to want him, but my body betrays me, melting as he speaks. He wants me still, even after he knows I was a whore. Bruiser seems to really like him, but if I leave, that means leaving Jazz and Rachel, and they won't have anyone.

"Most men run from me, yet here I am trying to run from you," I whisper.

"Stop running, I'll just chase you, and I will catch you to

love," he says, seductively. He moves quickly in front of me, removing my gun from my hand. I had forgotten I even had it still. He sets the gun down, then leans in closer, until our lips are almost touching. He smells amazing.

"Showken," I say, panting.

"Yes, zell?"

"Mmmm…"

"I know, I feel the same way, but you just say it, love," He says, licking his lips. "Tell me you will come home to our bed, and I will love you all night, giving us both pleasure."

My mind is racing. I want him so bad. Is it love or lust? I never had either, so I could be confused. I look into his eyes, and he is sure he loves me. I don't think I can stay away from this, this dragon man. Could I be truly in love?

SHOWKEN

Layern found me flying in circles, after throwing a serious tantrum ripping trees and scaring my people. He told me about Marilyn's reason for not believing she should be with me. I didn't waste any time going to see her. I'm not leaving without her. She's my Wella, my zell, and I don't want anything but her.

Now, standing this close to her body, I know she's mine. I want to make sweet love to her, but I need her to say she'll be mine. I know her body is aching for me, her arousal is hitting me like gusts of wind. She smells heavenly. She finally speaks.

"Showken, you're not from Earth. How could I fit in with you?" she breathes. I take a step back, and she steps forward, wanting me close.

"You would be my Wella, and therefore you would not have to worry about fitting in, as you say, you would be of me, that's enough, love," I say. She looks confused, finally moving to her sofa she flops down. I know that I'm asking more than a regular man, but I will give her more than any human man could.

"What about Bruiser?"

"He never wanted to leave the first time, of course he could come." I watch closely as she debates with herself over moving with me.

"I can't leave Jasmine and Rachel, no, I'm all she's got and she's all I got."

"You have me, beautiful," I say, raising a brow. "And if you won't leave without her then she's coming, because I'm not leaving without you." I can't believe I have to beg, but she's worth begging for. I need to figure out how to get her friend and Young into Cortamagen. I will worry about that later.

"I can't make that decision right now, besides you are not asking just me now, you want me to ask Jazz to come to an unknown place with dragons."

"Yes, and she will be fine," I respond calmly. I will not give up any more information about Jasmine coming. I must prepare the family first.

She stands and begins pacing back and forth. Bruiser and I both watch her, wondering what she will decide. I can't spend another night without holding her, she gives me comfort. She stops and stares at me for a long time.

"Showken, if I say yes," I say. My excitement is uncontrollable. "I have to bring Jasmine and Rachel, you already have agreed to Bruiser, right?"

"Yes, I agree."

"Wait, what do I say to Jazz, if she says no, I can't go. Listen, I'm not sure what you and I have, but if it doesn't work out, then you can't say I didn't try." She doesn't understand.

"Precious, once you accept being my Wella, you can never leave me, either we die together or live forever."

"Oh, wow, I didn't know that, does that mean Jazz and the baby would be there too, forever?"

"Yes."

"What's a Wella?"

"It's what humans call wife, but it's a little more intense in my world."

"So you saying if I agree, not only I can't ever leave, but neither can Jazz and Rachel?"

"Yes, but it's a great place and they would love it and the Young would be fine." I hope I'm doing a good job; Marilyn is good at guarding her emotions. We stare at each other for a second.

"So, what do we do now?"

"Baby, we go home, you, me and Bruiser. I will send for Jazz and the Young." I move closer to her. Bruiser's head lifts up and a loud bark escapes his mouth. I smile at him. He loves Cortamagen, I think he's found a friend to run with.

"Well, I need to take a shower and pack Bruiser's favorite toys, my pictures and some other things I would like to bring."

"Ok, let me help you zell, I can't wait to get you back home."

"You know that, all these sweet names you call me, you don't have to do that any more."

"Ohh my sweet, beautiful, precious zell, I will always and forever call you sweet names." I can't resist, and I go to her, lifting her to my face and giving her a long overdue soft deep kiss. I feel her legs wrap around my waist as she slides her hands into my hair, pulling hard. We finally get our composure. I can't wait to get her back home. We both begin to run around the house, packing everything she thinks she wants.

***

We finally make it back home. My smile can't get any wider. I feel like the happiest man alive. I can now understand Draken's love for Cess. I thought he was a fool to love so deep, but my love for Marilyn is a consuming fire that won't die.

I get her all unpacked, make sure Bruiser eats some food, and run my future Wella a bath. I tell Layern and Gemi to get the party ready to announce my future Wella. Once I have done all that, I walk into the bathroom to find her sleeping. I slip out of my pants, and climb into the bath with her.

"Hmmm…" Marilyn's eyes remain closed. She smiles. I lean over and kiss each closed eye.

"Beautiful, come here," I say, leaning back. She opens her eyes and pulls herself towards me. I help her straddle my lap.

"Better?"

"Love, it's much better, I feel as if you might disappear. I love you so much."

"I love you too, and I can feel you growing, Showken, under me." Her tongue comes out of her mouth, licking her beautiful, perfect lips. I can't wait any longer, I cup my hands on the sides of her face and start to kiss my Wella.

She wraps her hand around my erection and guides me into her sweet body. She moans "ohhh!" I love that sound. My eyes are drawn to her breast, as I'm taking my time to enjoy all of her.

"Yes, please, Showken," she cries out. I love the sound of my name on her lips. We find a rhythm in no time. Her body clenches my sex, she's like a tailored glove for me only. This is my body, forever.

"You feel so good, zell."

"Harder!"

"You need to walk tomorrow."

"Ahhh!!" She meets me with each thrust. She pulls my hair as I continue to kiss her body, enjoying her neck, shoulders and lips. Marilyn finds her release. "SHOWKEN!!!" I follow her soon after. We remain in place, loving each other. She rests her head on my chest, exhausted. I climb out, holding her, and take her to bed, letting her sleep.

I slip on a pair of loose pants and go in search of Layern. I find him in the kitchen, flirting with the cooks. I'm so happy my brother is back.

"Brother, is everything in place?" I ask. Layern nods, not taking his eyes off the pretty blonde. Layern can be bad, like I used to be. "Layern, five minutes, then you can go back to your fun," I say. He turns and looks at me.

"Oh brother, I've missed females. Marilyn sleeping?"

"Yes," I smile.

"Well, I've informed the entire family, everyone is a little skeptical, given that she did leave our land once. Cess is very happy, though, that means Draken is happy."

"He is totally whipped."

"So are you, my brother."

"This is true, and I love it. Make sure to calm Beauka. She's not too nice to anyone who she feels might hurt a family member."

"This is true, but Cess can handle Beauka, and she knows our jealous brother would rip her to shreds over Cess,"

"I see your point, send Cess to calm the storm our sister may have brewing."

"Mother did want to speak with you, but our father said no, that you made your decision and she would live with it."

"I don't believe you, Father would never disagree with Mother."

"Oh, brother, he did, so you owe Father." I'm not sure what to say, and shake my head in disbelief. I will not rattle my brain trying to figure this out. In due time I will find out her reasons for not wanting the ceremony between me and Marilyn.

"I'm going to go back to my room, going to grab a couple of trays of fruit and some wine." I smile, and see the servant smiling at Layern. "I see, brother, you will be having your own fun, too," I say, taking the trays that are laid out for me, as the servant heard me speak. I walk out with the fruit and wine, going back to Marilyn. Draken is there, waiting smiling. I open the door, set down the food and wine and step back out.

"Draken, stop smiling at me."

"Ohh, this is not a smile, it's a smirk. You thought I was a fool, now here you are, can't even leave your Wella alone for more than ten minutes."

"Really? The crazy jealous dragon that has issues with any man touching his Wella. Until I can give my sister Cess a hug without fearing your fire, you can't smirk." I see Bruiser coming down the hall, I open the door for him, and he goes inside to Marilyn. He loves her too. Draken eyes the dog as he passes.

"You're right, I do have issues with anyone touching Cess who has a penis, but I really would like to know why the dog?"

"Marilyn loves Bruiser, and he's grown on me, too, so don't frighten him. Have you figured out how to get Marilyn's friends here?"

"They are here, I have to admit when Layern told me she wanted them to come, I didn't think it was a good idea,"

"Marilyn loves them, and that was a condition of her coming back."

"Well, she'll be here soon. I sent Domlen and Gemi to pick her up."

"Shit, you haven't met her, Domlen is more than likely to piss her off."

"That's why Gemi went, the others would not go. You know they think Earth stinks."

We both laugh, because we did too at one time, well I did, but I enjoyed the women, so the smell never stopped me from going to Earth. I give Draken a hug and he departs, I'm sure to find his Wella. I hear Marilyn moving around in the bed and I go in to greet her. I slip into bed. Bruiser has found sleep. He looks so peaceful. I will give Marilyn and Bruiser a surprise. I smile to myself.

"Hi!" she says.

"Hello, Beautiful, are you hungry?"

"Yes, umm, where's Bruiser at?

"He's sleeping, I fed him and turned him loose to run freely in the garden," I say, slipping out of the bed and getting the tray.

"You are so handsome, Showken." Where did that come from? I will take the compliment, though. I give her a smile as I press a slice of pineapple to her lips. She opens her mouth and my body wants her again. She's sore; I will let her rest for a little while.

"Thank you, Beautiful, have some wine, it will go great with the fruit."

"Is Jazz here yet?"

"They are on their way."

"So she agreed?"

"I believe so, Draken said she's on her way and he never lies." I place a piece of kiwi fruit in my mouth, and then I lean to kiss Marilyn so I can share this delicious fruit with her.

"What happens now?"

"Well, tomorrow there's a party to celebrate our union, and two days later we marry."

"That fast huh, wow."

"I would marry you right now if I could, but a ceremony must take place, besides the people need to meet another princess that is coming into the family."

"Ohh, no baby, I don't need to be called a princess, Marilyn or Mari is just fine with me." I do not pay attention to anything she says, except she called me baby.

"I'm your baby, zell?"

Her grey eyes sparkle with joy. "Yes, you are my baby."

I bend and gently kiss her neck.

***

The day of the announcement of our union is today. I leave her a note as she sleeps, I have a dress picked out for her, hanging on a hook. My brothers will come for her soon. I give her another kiss, then beckon Bruiser to follow me. He turns and looks at her. He loves his owner. I go and get ready for the party.

MARILYN

I feel so good. This bed is so big and comfortable. I haven't seen Jazz, yet, I hope she's at the party. I took my bath early, after Showken and I had had more fun exploring each other's bodies. I climb out of bed and notice Bruiser is not around. I see the prettiest green gown I've ever seen. It's long and flowing. Wow, it's so pretty. I finally notice the note on the table, next to food and juice. It reads:

Beautiful, I'm so happy to have you and excited to show you off. It's tradition for my brothers to bring you to the party, but I will be waiting for you, in fact I will smell you first. Please don't give them a hard time about this, love, its tradition, and I can't

break it, so put on the gown, I know there are no shoes, you don't
need them here.

I love you and can't wait to see you in the dress.
I picked it out personally.
Showken

Damn, he has gorgeous handwriting. I swallow hard. He
mentioned about me becoming a princess yesterday. I don't want a
title, being with him is enough. I hope to see Jazz and Rachel
today, I miss them. I begin to get ready, not knowing what time
they will come for me. I quickly eat some food, trying to ease my
nervousness. I look for the panties and bras I packed, but they are
gone. I go through my things three or four times before I notice a
note on the floor by the dresser.

Beautiful, you won't need panties or bras either.
Showken.

Well, I'll be damned, he stole my underwear. I can't help but
laugh. I put the dress on and it fits perfectly. I feel like a princess
in this gown. I finish my makeup just as two knocks break the
silence. I go to the door and see all these fine ass men, wearing
nothing but loose pants - all in different colors, though.

"Hello, Marilyn, you look gorgeous," Draken says.

"Thank you," I say, blushing. They are all staring at me.

"We will surround you as you walk, I will lead you to

Showken, and he's waiting for you impatiently," Draken chuckles. I hear a growl. My eyes widen.

"Ohh don't worry, Marilyn, the growl is for us, not you," Layern says.

"Besides, I'm sure he gives you a different growl," Hawken says, smiling. I'm smiling myself. I've never been embarrassed around men before, but all of them like this is very intimidating. The other brothers laugh, and I feel really shy.

"Well, which way?"

"It doesn't matter, we will still get you to Showken," Domlen says. I shake my head at this fairy tale, and make a right down the hall. I feel very important with them walking with me. They are silent now. I notice crowns on their heads, shit they are princes. We come to the biggest doors I've ever seen and they open. WOW! It's tons of people everywhere. What kind of party is this? That's when I see Jazz and Rachel, all dressed up and waving at me. I wave back, smiling. We start to walk up some stairs and I see Showken's mother, and, I'm assuming, his father. Cess is dressed in a gorgeous purple gown. I start my search for Showken, and finally spot him at the end of this stage. His slacks match my dress. His chest looks amazing. I love him. Layern turns and smiles at me. Shit, did I say it out loud? I see Showken smiling at me, and those dimples are making me wet.

"Marilyn, control, we all can sense your arousal for our brother," Layern says. I notice they are all smiling extremely widely right now. Damn it. I don't say anything. We finally get to the top, and they all disperse to seats farther back. Showken and Bruiser come walking towards me. I smile, seeing Bruiser. He runs towards me, and I bend down and hug him tight. He's been the only thing that has kept me going for so long. I stand, and Showken is there with a sweet smile. He gets down on one knee in front of everyone. The silence is thick in the air.

"Marilyn Carrington, would you accept the responsibility of moving forward to become my Wella, forever?" he says, looking at me with those eyes.

"Yes," I say. The crowd erupts into clapping.

"Thank you, beautiful, now I present you with this ring, made for you," he says, as he pulls a ring from behind him. It's a green dragon. Wow, I'm really going to marry a dragon.

"Oh, Showken, I love you, at first I wasn't sure if it was lust, but at this moment I know that I love you." I say, as tears begin to fall. I hear Jazz yell out.

"That's what I'm talking about!"

I smile, knowing I have interrupted some kind of tradition. Showken holds the ring up for me. I hold out my hand and he places it on my finger. I notice it starts to move into a solid stone that looks like the hugest emerald.

"Marilyn, you are my everything, this ring is yours, protecting you when I'm not around." He stands. "I think you were mine when you first told me 'so fucking what'- I wanted you then." He smiles.

"I can't even remember that, now," I say. He leans in close.

"You smell amazing, but we are not quite done. My brothers are going to say something now." They have all gathered by us now. The spotlight has to end soon, I can't take all this attention.

The brothers speak to Showken.

"In this time of celebration, we, the Draglen brothers, promise to protect your future Wella until you are joined as one." They look at me. "We promise to watch over you and protect you until you are one with our brother, Prince Showken Draglen. Do you accept our help, Marilyn Carrington?"

I look at them, taking it all in, then finally I say:

"Yes, I will accept your help, unless you get on my nerves." I smile at Showken. He knows me and still wants me. I feel so special. They all laugh, and the crowd erupts in more applause and music, they are dancing and really partying now.

"Love, I'm going to go fly with my brothers, celebrating us, you will see me transform into a dragon, are you ok with that?" I bite my lip, I've never seen him transform into a dragon before.

"Well, umm, yes, I can do this." I say, feeling confident.

"Ok, one brother must stay behind to help you through this, whom do you choose?" he asks, leaning in for a kiss. My body warms instantly.

"I choose Layern," I say, looking up at him.

"You have such beautiful eyes," he says giving me another peck. "I enjoyed the grey, but the green I adore." His brothers are in the field waiting for him. Layern comes and stands by me. I wish Jazz could come, but she is still sitting, so it must be a tradition thing. Wait, did he say green eyes? My eyes are grey.

"No, they are green now," Layern says. "Once you accepted to be his Wella, they changed to green."

"I need to see a mirror," I say.

"You need to watch Showken change," Layern says, looking down at me. They are all so tall. "Are you nervous about seeing him change?"

"Yes, I am, but they are all going to change, that's going to be a lot of dragons." Layern lets out a laugh, making me smile too. For some reason I look towards the field and see Showken, smiling at me. I hold my breath as he begins to change. His body starts expanding, his pants rip apart, arms are stretched out in front of him. His hands begin to get longer and wider, and all the while his entire body is turning green, it's amazing. I'm still a little frightened, but I know it's Showken and he wouldn't harm me, the others I'm not sure.

"You're safe, Marilyn." He looks at Jasmine as she and Rachel watch them change too. "Your friend, she's intrigued with us, not afraid, interesting."

I raise a brow at Layern. Jazz is not a toy.

"I won't bed your friend, Marilyn, you have my word, some of my other brothers, if she's willing." He smiles. She is in this land now, Jazz will more than likely be with a dragon too. Layern is smiling. Showken is in the sky, looking amazing. They are pretty aggressive with each other in the sky. They are even shooting fire towards one another.

"Layern, they're not fighting, are they?"

"No, just brotherly love," he says, proudly. We both continue to watch until I see Showken coming back down to the ground. I have the urge to touch him. I take a step forward, and I lock eyes with him as a dragon. He lowers his body down as close to the ground as he can.

"Can I go up to him?"

"Well, normally the future Wella would wait behind, but Showken has positioned himself for you, so I say, go to your prince." I smile at hearing that, and move quickly towards him, I stop as I see a brown dragon coming down, but he spots me and turns and goes back into the air. Shit, who was that? I move closer to Showken, who is watching me closely. I finally reach him. He closes his eyes, and I reach out my hand to touch him. His skin is smooth and hard.

"You're beautiful, Showken, even in this huge beast body," I say, smiling. I take a risk, and lean down and kiss his skin. A loud growl leaves his mouth. His eyes open, and the same amazing green eyes are peering at me. I feel a gentle hand touch me.

"Marilyn," Cess says, pulling me away. "Unless you want us all to see Showken transform, and have his way with you in the field, no kissing the beast in public, they become very aroused."

"How do you know this, you're human like me?"

"Yes, I am, but I'm the Wella to Draken, and from personal experience, once the beast is aroused, when they transform they will have you." She smiles as if remembering a pleasurable event.

"He will come for you in a few minutes; he will transform soon, let's get some food, you will need the energy."

"Yes, I think you're right!" I say, walking up the stairs with Cess. We sit and are served with all sorts of food. Everything looks so pretty. I wave Jazz and Rachel over to sit with me. I see Bruiser in the field with Showken, running around him. Jazz takes a seat.

"Well, Princess Marilyn, when were you going to tell me you were dating a freaking dragon?" She grins. I love her so much, like a sister. There's no way I could be here without her.

"Don't call me that, Jazz, I'm still Mari."

"You is crazier than a rolling lizard, you in a freaking castle marrying a dragon prince, bitch you a princess." Cess looks at Jazz, like is everything ok.

"Cess," I say. "This is my best friend Jasmine and her daughter Rachel, excuse Jazz for her comments. There is no filter between her mouth and her brain."

"Oh, you are the one Domlen and Gemi went to get. I was going to come introduce myself, but Draken is a very sexual man. Marilyn, I'm sure you have encountered the distracting effect they can have on you." Cess grins. She's such a beautiful lady, she looks like this is the right place for her.

"Yes, I have encountered Showken's distractions, and they are amazing." I giggle. I can't believe I just giggled. I haven't giggled, wait, I can't even remember giggling.

"Well, I want a distraction too, how the hell do I get a dragon too?" Jazz says, drinking her wine.

"You don't get them," Cess says. "If you get the attention of a Draglen brother, you will know instantly." We continue to eat and talk. I'm having a good time. I feel extremely happy right now. I see a hand stretched out in front of me, and I know it's Showken. He has a wrap on now. Oh my, he's freaking naked.

"Showken," Jazz says. "This is a really nice place, I think I'm going to like this place."

"Well, I'm happy you like it here, Jasmine, make yourself at home, just watch out for my brothers, they love sex." He smiles at me.

"Beautiful, you ready to take a walk with me?" I glance at Cess and she's smiling like 'get ready'. I nod, taking his hand and walking away from the party. We walk in silence, and soon we end up at a beautiful bench covered in flowers and jewels, it's unreal.

"I thought we could have some time alone, they will party all night, precious," he whispers. His eyes are watching my every move. I notice a picnic setting about ten feet away, as I walk around the bench. I glance at Showken, who is smiling at me. He has done this for me. I fall more in love with him.

"Showken, you are so romantic, our own personal picnic. I love it," I say, getting closer. I see meats, veggies, fruit, nuts, and… cupcakes. Showken comes up behind me, wrapping his strong arms around me, kissing my neck. This feels so good, I think.

"I usually eat lots of food after flying, and I thought maybe you wanted a cupcake or two."

"Or three, it looks like about ten cupcakes out here, Mister," I say, turning to face him. Before I can say another word, he attacks my lips. We are kissing roughly. I feel so connected to him now for some reason, then I remember Layern said my eyes were green now.

"Wait," I say, panting. "Are my eyes green?"

"Yes, zell. You didn't know?"

"No, I didn't, I want to see." He gives me a wicked smile.

"Ok." I'm not sure what he's up too, but Showken is going to find something to have fun with. We stare at each other for a few seconds, before I'm lifted into the air, moving at a speed that's unreal, before coming to a stop at a river. It's clear and pretty.

"You can see by just looking into the water, it's magic, love, you'll see. Lean over and look into the water."

"Showken, don't push me in the water, I'm not playing, I don't want to get wet."

"I think you like getting wet, in fact I like you wet," he smiles. "I promise I will not push you into the water, love, this is the closest place I could think of where you could see your beautiful eyes."

I narrow my eyes at him, giving him a warning about pushing me into the water. I like this dress. I lean over and the water circles until it's a mirror. I can see myself clearly. WOW!! My eyes are green, I can't believe it. I stare at myself in the water and can't believe it's me.

"I have green eyes!" I yell, happily. I touch my face

wondering how I look with them. "How do I look?"

"You look like my Wella," he smiles. "A beautiful princess for me. Come, food awaits us."

We go back to our picnic and eat, and laugh about how we met. I tell him about my past myself, we drink wine and have the best time ever.

"Showken, will it always be this magical?"

"I plan on making it magical for you forever."

"Really?" I squeal.

"Oh, yes, like right now I need about three or four of those cupcakes." He raises his brow. "The frosting needs to be off, do you have an idea where I can put that?"

"Ohh, my sexy dragon is seducing me?"

"I'm trying, maybe you should come out of that dress."

"Outside, right now, what if-"

"Don't worry, we are all alone, you, me and cupcakes." We both laugh. Showken is so easy to love. He is truly a fun, lovable dragon. I forget he's a dragon sometimes, until he growls. He crawls towards me like the predator he is, hovering over me.

"I need you out of that dress, zell."

"I like this dress, besides we are outside."

"I see, you are going to be difficult." He places his hands on my hips, and I feel a burning coming through the dress, it doesn't hurt, but feels like I'm about to have an orgasm.

"You don't play fair," I glare. He laughs, capturing my mouth, we are all over each other and in no time his wrap is off. He throws it over his shoulder.

"See, love, if I'm going bare, so are you." He gives me no chance as he gets the dress off, in spite of my resistance. He has two cupcakes in each hand, oh my.

"I really love my cupcakes," he says, smearing the frosting all over my body. We are no longer laughing, but panting. My body is yearning for him. My nipples get hard underneath all the frosting, and Showken makes his way to my doodah. After I'm covered in multiple flavors, he pulls my legs apart. "Time for me to eat my frosting, zell." I blush as I feel his hot tongue licking, biting, and sucking the frosting off my body.

"Showken, I need… "

"I'm still eating my frosting, love," he chuckles, and he goes back to my clitoris, sucking hard until I come loudly.

"OHHH, YESS!!!" It's not long before he's inside me, thrusting in and out. There is no sound but our bodies rubbing against one another. This is more than a fairy tale, this is a dream I'm living. We continue our lovemaking for the rest of the evening, enjoying each other.

SHOWKEN

Marilyn and I lie comfortable in our bed. After making love several times, she fell asleep, and I vanished us to our bed. It's only a day and a half until she is officially my Wella. Her eyes are green, which almost completes her transformation. Layern took care of Bruiser last night. I climb out of the bed slowly, and leaving my zell in bed to sleep, I shower and leave the room to get ready for the ceremony. I shield my room, as I don't want anyone coming to kidnap my Wella. Draken should have thought of that too. I walk to the kitchen to put in a special order for tomorrow, and after that I go to my art room to draw Marilyn a picture. I've never been this happy. I'm drawing when I smell Velca coming close to my door. What does she want? I get up and open the door before she knocks.

"Oh, Showken, sometimes I forget how well we all can smell, being dragons," she says, entering the room uninvited.

"What do you want, Velca?" I narrow my eyes. I'm still not sure why Draken keeps her alive, I don't like her.

"Well, I know this is bad timing, but you taking this human as your Wella is going to look really bad for Cortamagen."

"Velca," I growl. "I'm about to forget you're a female, leave, now."

She takes a seat on my bench.

"I never wanted to marry Draken," she says, softly. "I always thought you and I would be a better fit, I mean being a queen someday does not impress me."

I glare. "I would never have you, not even if I were single, which I'm not." I summon Layern and Domlen to come to my art room before I kill Velca.

"I'm not saying that you should have me. I'm simply saying, though I saved Cess' life. The people in the land are wondering, why are the Draglen descendants taking humans as their Wellas?" She stands as she senses Domlen and Layern coming.

"Velca, if anything goes wrong tomorrow, anything, if the sun doesn't shine bright enough, I'm going to rip your head off your body."

"Oh Showken, you know I don't do violence."

Layern and Domlen crowd the door as she tries to leave.

"Excuse me," Velca says.

"Have a seat" Domlen demands. Draken comes barreling into the room and Velca jumps trembling into the corner.

"VELCA," he yells. "You live because of my Wella, and you are trying to start trouble. Do you want to leave the castle, because you will lose our protection, many would love to impress me with your head on a platter."

"Draken, I, I-"

"You are just leaving." Draken towers over her. She runs out of the room in tears. I just want to rip her head off her body. My brothers dismiss Velca's weak attempt to start trouble. We all know she wants to be a princess, but none of us will ever marry her.

"Brother, don't worry about a thing," Draken says. "Nothing will interfere with your day. You have my word." Layern and Domlen both nod and we all head out of the room. We go for a quick flight. I'm pissed off that Velca thinks she can ever scare me away from Marilyn. Where did that come from? The only logical reason comes to mind, Mother. After the flight I go for a run with Bruiser, letting him catch me this time, and we both find food. I play with him, understanding how Marilyn loves him so much. I decide that I need to pay my mother a visit. I find her in the garden, a favorite place for her.

"Hello, my son, something you would like to ask?" I just stare at her. How could she send Velca to me like that? "I take it Velca came to see you, and you think I sent her."

"Yes," is my only response. I'm pissed.

"I didn't send her, but I knew she would find a way to be alone with you." I start breathing hard, feeling steam leaving my body. I'm becoming more aware of how angry I am. "You need to calm down, wouldn't want you crisp for your big day, my son." She glares. I take a few deep breaths.

"Now, Velca is concerned with securing herself a place within this family, she feels overlooked. I will ensure she doesn't mess up your day, but one of you will have to marry her, or kill her.

"I vote kill."

"Of course you do. She will be contained, but if you and your brothers don't want her, send her out of the castle."

"Cess thinks she's a friend."

"She is a friend," Mother says, standing. "Until she finds that my sons don't want her. She will become a wounded animal. It will become unsafe in the castle for your Wellas with her living here." She walks over to me. "Everything will be fine, now on to more pressing business. Beauka will cause a scene if you don't introduce her to your future Wella." She leans to give me a kiss. I relax.

"Thank you, Mother, and I'll get Marilyn to Beauka today."

"Great, see you tomorrow." She disappears right in front of me. If Velca wants to be a part of this family she will be waiting for a long time, no brother will touch her, though she's a virgin, maybe one of the brothers will find her attractive enough to bed, but never take her as a Wella.

I continue to get tomorrow ready for Marilyn. Finally I come back to the room and find her reading. She is reading a family book of our history, completely naked. I love her body, and it's all mine.

"Showken, how many kids do you want?"

"Hello, Beautiful, trying to find out more history, interesting," I say.

"Yes, like the fact most have eight or more Youngs, Showken I'm not having that many kids."

"Oh, love, don't worry, it will be so much fun making them." She shakes her head and comes towards me with that beautiful bare body. I like this mood she's in.

"Well," she smiles. "I woke and you were gone, and I missed you, so I started to go through your things and found the book, but if you had been here when I woke, we would be having a very different discussion right now."

"As bad as I want you right now, my sister wants to meet you, and with Beauka it's best just to get her out of the way."

"Well, ok, I saw her yesterday. She looks really quiet." She starts to put on a dress. "Hey, I haven't seen Jazz or Rachel, are they ok? I thought she would be on our doorstep this morning banging for us to let her in."

"She was doing something this morning," I say, smiling. Marilyn turns and looks shocked.

"No, please say Jazz didn't sleep with one of your brothers."

"Jazz didn't sleep with one of my brothers," I say, laughing. I am bound by brother to brother.

"Showken-"

"Love, my sister is waiting, now listen, whatever you do, don't drink her tea," I say. My little sidetrack worked.

"Her tea, well I don't like tea anyway, but why?"

"You don't want to know," I say, as she buttons the dress. I really like this dress too. We visit with Beauka for a few hours, and it seems like they get along great. Marilyn loves our time there, and Beauka sends a message to my head letting me know she approves. I smile, knowing this day is ending and tomorrow evening Marilyn will be my Wella forever.

MARILYN

I can't believe I have puked five times today. I'm getting ready to become a Wella to Showken, who I love a lot, but marriage. I feel like I need to puke again.

"Mari, stop puking, that's just gross, now lick some of this salt." Jazz frowns as she pours some into my hand. I notice Queen Nala and Beauka at the door. "If you just going to stand there then you can go have a seat, I have to get her prepared to marry Showken." Jazz frowns at them both.

"Marilyn, you need to get dressed, your gown is all already for you. Beauka is going to do your hair," Showken's mom says.

"When pigs fly. I'm doing her hair, I'm her best friend."

"Yes, but she's becoming my sister."

"Bitch, back off, I'm doing her hair, dragon or not I will kick your ass all around this room." Oh shit, not today, Jazz.

"I will do my own hair," I say, glaring at them both. "Both of you better not ruin my day with this arguing." I wish I had my gun, I would have shot a warning in the air.

"Fine, Mari," Jazz says. "Only for you."

"Well, we have forever to get to know each other, sister," Beauka smirks.

"You don't want to dance with me."

"Enough!" Queen Nala yells.

I ignore them and go over to my dress. It's fit for a princess. It's full of jewels. They all help me get this dress on as it has an extremely long train. The dress is off one shoulder, with splits on both sides. I notice as I walk to do my makeup that these splits are right up to my ass. What kind of gown is this? Whatever. I'm completely ready now. We all look in the mirror. Everyone is smiling, including me.

"Well, our work here is done, Marilyn," Showken's mother says. "You will walk to the ceremony by yourself." I look at Jazz and she looks at me. Why?

"I don't know my way around the castle."

"You will do fine," Beauka says, trying to convince me. I roll my eyes.

"Get Showken here right now, I'm not walking by myself." I sit on the bed.

"Well," his mother says. "My son got a very determined one. We will all leave and I'll send Showken." They leave the room. I stand, feeling a little pissed. I don't want to walk by myself, why can't one of his brothers walk with me? I'm not going to do it. I hear a knock on the door. I go and open, but nobody's there.

"Hello, zell."

"Showken," I plead. "I'm not walking alone, come get me."

"I'm walking with you, love, just trust me,"

"No, come get me now!" I yell.

"You are yelling, love, everyone can hear, trust me please."

"How do I get there?"

"Follow my voice and the feeling you get."

"Showken, I'm scared."

"Me too, I have never done this either."

"Shit, you could get me lost then." I hear him laugh.

"It's not funny."

"I know, love, please trust me."

"Ok, ok, but if I get lost I'm going to be so pissed at you."

"You are so beautiful, come," he says, and my body turns left and start walking.

"I didn't expect to fall in love, precious."

"I didn't either."

"Yet, you stole my heart, from the first sight."

"You annoyed me at first sight." I laugh, continuing to walk.

"I fell in love with you, love,"

"I fell in love with you too."

"We will always be together, love."

"You will never leave me."

"I will never leave you," I come to some doors. "Come through the doors, beautiful."

"Ok." I open the door and there are people everywhere. Some are smiling, some have tears in their eyes. My eyes fill with tears as I see how beautiful everything looks. A girl who was nothing but a whore is now going to be a princess. I guess dreams do come true.

"Come forth, love," Showken says. I turn and see him standing on a stage again. He begins to walk towards me. I have to walk up these stairs with this sexy ass dress, my ass might fall out. I take my time coming up, until we are face to face on the steps. I feel shy and glance down, looking at this pretty dress I'm wearing. He takes my hand and walks me up the stairs until we reach the top. I see Jazz crying, and then I spot Bruiser on the stage. I smile.

"Turn towards the crowd, my love, let the people see my princess." I turn, and people give me smiles and nods. This is so weird.

"I need you to trust me," He looks at me strangely, and looks around like he hears something. I frown, wondering what's going on. He locks eyes with me. He gets a huge grin on his face.

"You are with my Young!" he says.

"What, no, Showken, people are looking." He places his hand on my stomach and closes his eyes.

"Yes, you are, the heartbeat is strong." He pulls me into a hug, holding me tight. I'm pregnant, already. I close my eyes. "I love you, Wella," he says. Bruiser comes and stands beside me. Then a warming feeling starts to build within me.

"Showken, what's happening?"

"Trust me, close your eyes."

"I want to see." We stare at each other a few seconds.

"Ok."

The warming feeling turns really hot, and I see fire transferring from Showken to me. My eyes widen as it closes around us, and I look down and see Bruiser inside the fire. It's not burning us. Showken pulls my face to his.

"I love you."

"I love you more," I say. We kiss, and the fire gets hotter. Something is happening to me. We stare at each other as the green fire circles all three of us. Finally the warming feeling goes down, and so does the fire. The crowd erupts into clapping and dancing, music. I'm rushed by Jazz, Cess and Beauka.

"You knocked up?" Jazz says.

"I'm so happy for you," Cess says. "This is great."

"The next generation of Draglens is officially started," Beauka says.

I'm in shock, I can't speak. Showken never releases my hand. Pulling me over to his father, he too places his hand on me.

"Yes, she's carrying a Draglen," Showken's dad says. "Congratulations, my daughter, and welcome to the family." I look at Showken, who is looking at me in amazement. Queen Nala smiles at me. The brothers all come to touch my stomach. Finally, Showken turns to the crowd.

"Attention, my people, a new Draglen will be born soon, to my Wella, she carries a Young!" He excites the crowd and they go wild. I step closer to him.

"Beautiful, you look amazing, your hair, eyes, everything, now you have my Young. You hungry?"

"You are such a sweet kind dragon."

"Yes, well, I'm going to change so we can go."

"We not staying here?"

"Ohh no, I'm taking you to a special place, to eat and to make love to my Wella, my pregnant Wella."

He walks me down the stairs, and two brothers follow, I'm sure one is called Warton, the other is Layern. We stop in the field as Showken changes before my eyes, and I feel awesome, knowing he's all mine. I rub my belly, wondering what it will be like to carry a dragon.

"Come, Marilyn, we will help you up."

"I'm to ride on top of Showken?"

"Yes," Warton says. He seems mean.

"Ok." We get to Showken, and Layern lifts me up until I'm around his neck. The dress is perfect; my train is spread across his back and my legs are hanging.

"Hold on tight," Layern says, I smile and Showken lifts up in the air, and it feels so free. I laugh out loud as we fly away. I turn and notice Bruiser has blond hair now, with piercing green eyes. I love Showken, I lean over and say.

"Thank you for this wonderful day, my dragon," I chuckle. I hold on as he speeds away.

***

We land on a huge cliff covered in grass. It's so beautiful. He changes back into human form. He puts his wrap on walking towards me.

"I have a big surprise for you," he says, walking me into the forest away from the cliff. We come to a stop. There's a home just ahead. It looks huge.

"It's small, only 15 rooms, but it will be our private oasis when we need time to ourselves away from everyone." He bends and kisses my belly. "I didn't expect a Young so soon," he says. "But this home will come in handy for all our Youngs."

"You're giving me a castle?"

"Well, I'm going to be there too." He smiles.

"Come, let's eat." he says, turning me to a table full of everything one could desire. He turns me again, and there are three long tables filled with huge cupcakes.

"Plan on keeping me here for some time, huh?"

"Oh I plan on keeping you forever, my beautiful Wella." I turn, and give him a kiss that starts the warming feeling, maybe food will wait.

Thank you for taking the time to read SHOWKEN, the second book in the Draglen Brothers series. Please enjoy the first chapter of the next book, "LAYERN."

LAYERN

I should never have put my life on hold for her. Now that I'm back to myself, I'm catching up with as many females as I can. Five years, shit, I will never go that long without sex again. I love sex. It's the best part of life. I've always had the upper hand with any female I take to bed.

Now that Showken has a Wella, he can't go on the hunt with me for new women, so I have enlisted Gemi and Fewton. They are always happy to please women like I do. I'm glad we are taking a break from Earth. Father wants all the family around Marilyn, since she's carrying the first Draglen descendent for the next generation. He's very cautious about things of this nature. I'm sure

Cess will be with Young soon, also. Well, I have been waiting for Gemi and Fewton for a few minutes now, we are flying to a neighboring land, Noke. It's filled with beautiful female dragon-shifters, plus it's where Malio lives. She and I were in love, or I was in love with her.

I wanted her to be my Wella until I found she had been with another dragon-shifter, my cousin. After killing him, I could not stand to look at her. I took a vow of celibacy until my love no longer belonged to her. I'm hoping to let her see how happy I can be without her. When I look over my shoulder, I spot Gemi and Fewton.

"What took so long?" I ask, studying them. I'm the brother you can't lie to. I would know. Though I don't do exact predictions, I'm usually right. The gift I have is hard to explain, I received it from my mother's side of the family. My gift is not as strong as Mother's; I can't predict the future as well as she can, but feelings, thoughts, I'm pretty good with that, especially with dragons, humans are more complex at times, but over time I can break down what they are hiding, too.

"Gemi has been playing with some of the servants," Fewton says. As they reach me, I feel myself getting excited. Lately I can't stop myself from wanting female company. I really deprived myself far too long.

"Well, I'm ready to change into our dragons so we can go," I say. My brothers nod in agreement, and we spread out to give ourselves room as we change. My dragon is blue, Mother says because I have the gift of Joha, or moods of knowing. We all change and fly to Noke.

***

Making it there in good time, we transform back into human form, in a field that is reserved for just the Draglen family. The servants are there waiting with wraps for us.

"Ok, brothers, I am pretty sure I hear music, which means sexy dancing dragon females," I say, sniffing the air. "It also seems we have a few other species out to play, mermaids and fairies." I smile, remembering how much fun they can be.

"Layern," Gemi says. "I'm glad you are back. I thought you would stay celibate."

Fewton is too busy walking towards the music even to think about what we are saying. Fewton loves women just as much as I do. Gemi likes to please them, but he wants a Wella. The music gets louder, and I can hear the singing. This is going to be a fun night. Fewton has found a few females to play with. Gemi looks at me.

"I'll see you in the morning?" he asks. I smile, and nod. None of us currently has a Giver. We like variety, but sometimes we take a Giver just so we don't have to seduce. Gemi heads over to the garden, where a group is drinking and dancing. I'm one of the best dancers among my brothers. Making a female of any species orgasm during dancing is pleasurable for me. I see a couple of dragons eyeing me, I can even hear them speaking about me. "Prince Layern is here," one says. "Prince Layern, ohh, just to have one night." I walk their way. I can make their dream a reality.

Hello, lecenas," I say. Lecena means flower. In Kalin it's a great compliment to call a female a flower. They both smile, and I pull them to the middle of the dancing area. Everyone's body is twisting, turning, and grinding on one another. The music is sensual and sexy. The dragon females begin to dance with me. I squeeze the hips of the one with the golden eyes, as I pull her closer. The other one, with pink eyes, has her back to me as she dances, sliding up and down my body. We get a rhythm going and they are mush in my hands. I'm able to touch them any place I want. We kiss as we dance. I'm having fun when I spot a woman with red hair staring at me with piercing light orange eyes. She's a dragon, but not all the way. How can that be? The only half dragon is in Marilyn's stomach. The law allowing half dragons has only been approved in the last hundred years, so where did she come from? I have never seen her before. She walks with such grace and class. You would think she was royalty. I would have known it if this were the case, though. We know all the other royal families on this planet. I can no longer focus on the dragon women I'm dancing with; I must know who this dragon is. I let my gift seek for her, yet even though we are making eye contact, my gift is blocked. She smiles as if she knows. I give both dragons a kiss and walk straight for her.

"Hello."

"Hello," she replies back.

"Your name, please?" I ask.

"Prince Layern, I know who you are. You should know who I am." I hear the hurt in her voice. This woman is a mystery. I narrow my eyes. I don't like playing guessing games.

"You know who I am, good, then tell me your name."

She stares directly at me. We don't blink. She takes a deep breath, and gives me a smile.

"My name is Reseda, and I'm dragon and human, the first of my kind." She speaks with such pride. I know this cannot be true.

"Reseda, you lie." I snap. "The first of that kind will be born to my brother's Wella." I never get pissed, but her telling such a lie is disrespectful. I'm not sure what kind of magic she's playing with, but I do smell human cells within her body.

"I only speak the truth," she says, looking into my eyes. "You should ask Queen Nala who I am. She knows, as she banned me from Cortamagen." I'm thrown by her beauty. Her skin is flawless, her body is perfect and she's offended me.

"Keep the Queen, my mother, out of your speech," I say. "If she knew you spoke with such disrespect, she would have your head." This Reseda has me angry and aroused at the same time. I really want to lick her pretty skin. She looks and smells amazing.

"I don't care about your queen," she snaps. "Far as I can tell, she's an evil dragon."

Who the hell is this?

"Reseda," I say, stepping closer. "I'm not sure how many

passes I can give you, with that tongue of yours, you know I'm willing to overlook everything you said, and allow you to make it up to me, with that venomous tongue you have, all over my body." We are now only about an inch apart. I hear her heart beating faster. She looks a little shaken at what I just said.

"How dare you?"

"I do dare, do you accept?"

"No, you need to walk away from me." She glares and her eyes flicker. She's a dragon, alright.

"Reseda, this is getting serious, I came to Noke to find a dragon for the night, to please her, everywhere. Would you like that?" I ask, sliding my hands around her waist. I start moving her body with the beat of the music. She rolls her eyes, and begins to dance with me. I can't believe how good a dancer she is. Her body is all over me, I feel my sex rising as she brings a leg around my waist, holding me as she climbs my body, twisting her body sensually. She throws her head back, letting the dancing control her body, but not her mind. I find myself wanting her now. I run my hands up her body, letting her lead. She leans back as she lets her body continue the lovely moves. I smile, knowing she will be in a bed with me tonight. The music stops. She slides down my body. I look her in the eyes as she tries to break my hold.

"I have to go. My time is up." She pushes harder against me. I squeeze tighter.

"No, I like our time together, and I would like to continue to have more time with you in private."

"You don't understand, I have no choice, I sneak into Cortamagen. My time is limited before Queen Nala senses my presence."

"Reseda, you need to explain."

"Listen, I thought I could hate you, but I see now you don't know about me. You really don't want me, I'm not human, not dragon, in between species." She looks around. I keep my eyes on her. "I have to go, but it was nice to meet one of the Draglen brothers, I've only heard stories about you from my mother."

"Who is your mother?" I ask.

"She's the reason I sneak into Noke. My mother is nothing but a servant now, but at one time she and the queen were best friends."

"Reseda," I say. "This story you tell is getting even more outrageous. Come, I have a place where we can talk and sleep."

"Please let me go, I'm not what you think, and I will not do what you want."

"I'll let you go, Reseda, but you must promise to contact me when you come again." I lean to kiss her, and she turns her head.

"Ok, no kiss then. How old are you?"

"On Earth, I'm 24 years old; really I'm 310 years old. Now, I have to go," she pleads. I release her, and she turns, running in a full sprint, not as fast as dragons, but still very fast. She disappears in the night. I stand there for a minute, wondering what has just happened. I came here to have sex with some hot dragons, but now I have to get some answers. Reseda does have human blood, but she is dragon too. Her eyes changed in front of me, from human to her beast. 'Reseda, you are not going to get rid of me like that,' I think. I can't figure it out tonight. I glance over my shoulder and see the two dragon women, staring at me still hoping. I walk over to them.

"I would like to have you both, can I?" I ask. I already know they are willing to do anything to say they have had sex with a Draglen brother.

"Yes, we accept your offer, Prince Layern," the one with the pink eyes says. "And may we say it's an honor and a pleasure to be with you." I smile. Taking their hands, I lead them away to my place for the night. I will lose myself with these beauties for tonight, and in the morning I will go in search of Reseda. She will not get off that easily.

I hope you have enjoyed reading SHOWKEN and the first chapter of the next book, LAYERN!

Solease M Barner

Book 3 in the Draglen Brothers series

LAYERN

THE DRAGLEN BROTHERS SERIES

CONTACT

I love to connect with readers! Here is where you can find me.

https://www.facebook.com/TheDrakenBrothersASeriesBySolease
MBarner

https://www.facebook.com/solease.marksbarner

If you are interested in more works by Solease M Barner, checkout

https://www.facebook.com/TheSecretsOfTheGhostsTrilogy

OTHER SERIES BY SOLEASE BARNER

"Secrets of the Ghosts-The Sleeper"

"Secrets of the Ghosts-AWAKENS"

COMING SOON!

"Secrets of the Ghosts-REDEMPTION"

ABOUT THE AUTHOR

Solease lives in a quiet area. She is a wife, and mother to a daughter. Solease loves to spend time with her family. She's been called the social butterfly by many friends. She's a huge movie buff, and loves to read books. She writes poetry on a daily basis, as a way to release stress. Solease is the author of "Secrets of the Ghosts - The Sleeper", "Secrets of the Ghosts - AWAKENS", "The Draglen Brothers Series - DRAKEN" BK 1, and "The Draglen Brothers Series –SHOWKEN" BK 2

NOTE FROM THE AUTHOR:

Want to find out what happens next?

The next book in my series will be released later this year.

https://www.facebook.com/TheDrakenBrothersASeriesBySolease
MBarner

Prefer print?

A compilation of all books in the series are available in print.

Reviews are gold to authors! If you've enjoyed this book, would you consider rating it and reviewing it where your downloaded this ebook.

SOLEASE M BARNER

SECRETS

OF THE

GHOSTS

THE SLEEPER

SOLEASE M BARNER

SECRETS

OF THE

GHOSTS

BOOK 2

AWAKENS

Paradox Book Cover Design

Patti Roberts.

E: pattiroberts7@gmail.com

Solease M Barner

LAYERN
THE DRACLEN BROTHERS SERIES

Made in the USA
Las Vegas, NV
05 April 2023

70203403R00156